Annie's Quilted Mysteries™

A MIDSUMMER NIGHT'S SEAM

RACHAEL PHILLIPS

Annie's®
AnniesFiction.com

A Midsummer Night's Seam
Copyright © 2014 Annie's.

The characters and events in this book are fictional, and any resemblance to actual persons or events is coincidental.

Library of Congress-in-Publication Data
A Midsummer Night's Seam / by Rachael Phillips
p. cm.
I. Title
2013920283

AnniesFiction.com
800-282-6643
Annie's Quilted Mysteries
Series Creator: Shari Lohner
Series Editors: Shari Lohner, Janice and Ken Tate

10 11 12 13 14 | Printed in China | 9 8 7 6 5 4

All the world's a stage, and all the men and women merely players.

—William Shakespeare

one

"Be at the The Paddington, back door, no later than four forty-five." Emma Cotton's aunt, Dottie Faye Sinclair, hung up without another word.

As much as Emma loved her sixty-six-year-old aunt, part of her wished Dottie Faye hadn't invited herself along on this trip to New York. Emma, who had been fingering exotic silks in an exclusive Garment District store, tried to smooth away sudden wrinkles she felt forming in her forehead. Kelly Grace, co-owner of their small-town quilting shop, gave Emma's arm a sympathetic squeeze. "Dottie Faye's up to something."

"How did you guess?" Emma smiled, but she shook her head. "Dottie wants us to meet her behind The Paddington Theater in two hours."

"Do you think—?"

"Of course." Emma rolled her eyes. "She's hatched her own plan to snag Crawford."

Kevin Crawford, an up-and-coming off-Broadway actor/singer, wowed audiences and critics alike.

He also knew something about who had murdered their best friend Rose fifteen years ago—or he had killed her himself.

"I'd love to walk to the Theater District." Emma wanted to absorb the crisp November sunshine, a welcome change from the fabulous yet windowless fabric shops. "I need to clear my head before I deal with Dottie Faye."

Kelly consulted her phone. "We're within walking distance. Maybe we can grab a snack on the way?"

Kelly never faces a crisis on an empty stomach. Emma chuckled. How did her forty-something friend, with her endless appetite, keep her stomach so flat?

Two enormous pieces of New York cheesecake fueled their walk. The Garment District had fulfilled their dreams, but the Big Apple's noise and bustle never stopped. Skyscrapers blocked the sun. Emma wished she were back in Mystic Harbor, Massachusetts, where she could draw a deep breath without bumping someone's elbow.

Yet, neither she nor Kelly had considered this visit optional. They'd continue their "business trip" until the soiree after tonight's show. Emma's sorority sister Cat Simon, a theater-savvy magazine writer, had finagled a ticket for her. There she would meet Crawford face-to-face—the first step in dispelling the cover-up in Rose's case that she and Kelly only recently had discovered.

Somehow, they secretly had to collect Crawford's DNA to compare with the DNA found under Rose's fingernails after her "accident."

They'd tried the direct approach with earlier witnesses, only to snarl their case in a hundred ways. Emma groaned inwardly. With Dottie Faye involved, secrecy would prove a challenge. And if her aunt discovered she hadn't been invited to the soiree, she would go ballistic.

The scarlet-edged, snowy white awning of The Paddington Theater, a weathered brick building with elegant arched door-ways, met their eyes. Emma and Kelly ducked a small stream of emerging Wednesday matinee-goers and made a beeline for the theater's back entrance. Emma prayed they could intercept Dottie Faye before she grabbed Crawford.

Kelly gasped, and Emma followed her friend's gaze.

Emma's millionaire aunt, her big blond hair covered with an

even bigger, curlier black wig and paper hat, cheerfully manned the counter of a food truck. Dottie Faye wore a shocking pink uniform that emphasized her surprising curves. She slapped mustard, onions, and sauerkraut onto her creations as if she'd done it for years.

Catching sight of them, Dottie Faye called, "You pretty girls want a hot dog?" She slathered on a backwoods version of her accent the way she did Dijon mustard.

Emma swallowed. "We just ate cheesecake—"

"'Course you want one. My dogs are good for what ails you." She shoved two, loaded with onions, across the counter.

Kelly munched hers with gusto.

Emma nibbled. "These taste wonderful," she said carefully, "but when did you decide to be a hot dog vendor?"

"Last night. Best idea I've had yet. By this afternoon, I'd rented this outfit and set up shop." She gestured with her head toward The Paddington's back exit, where college-age girls clustered, ostensibly seeking autographs. "I'll fix Crawford a free hot dog and cola. You and Kelly follow him and fetch his disposables when he dumps them—DNA to go."

"Sounds great," Emma said, "but from all I've read, he's into health food. He might not want a hot dog—"

"'Course he will." Dottie Faye smiled into her silver compact's mirror. "After all that singing and acting, he'll be hungry as a hound dog."

"I hope you're right." Emma forced down another bite. She pictured a digestive smackdown at bedtime: cheesecake versus mustard and onions.

"I'll bet that's him." Dottie Faye's stage whisper turned Emma's gaze to the exit. Three men, one carrying a toolbox, hurried down the steps. Another wore a navy hoodie pulled over his eyes. The waiting girls paid little attention, but

Emma glimpsed the odd yet handsome face that adorned the enormous *A Midsummer Night's Dream* poster by the theater's front doors.

Dottie Faye left the truck and blocked Crawford's path. "Don't hurry off, sugar."

Emma pulled Kelly into a shop's alcove and peeked around the corner. If Dottie Faye's scheme didn't work—and Emma was sure it wouldn't—she didn't want Crawford to associate them with a psycho hot dog vendor.

"I made this free hot dog and cola just for you." Her aunt's cheery tones floated back to them.

"No thanks." Crawford brushed past Dottie Faye.

She maneuvered herself in front of him again. "Your mama wouldn't want you to go hungry, son."

"No *thank* you."

He sprinted away as passersby stared.

"Well, I never!"

Rushing up, Emma barely stopped her aunt from throwing the food at his retreating back as he disappeared into an alley.

"You'd think I'd tried to mug him." Dottie Faye slammed the food onto the counter.

Dots of cola and condiments decorated Emma's khaki coat. She counted to twenty and fought to drain the I-told-you-so tone. "I'm sorry you went to all this trouble."

Her aunt's blue eyes glittered. "He won't get away from me again."

Dabbing at multicolored spots, Emma knew Kelly felt her pain.

What new plan would Dottie Faye concoct to capture Crawford's DNA?

"That's him—sitting in the corner by himself." Emma's friend Cat, holding a martini, wiggled a pinky toward Kevin Crawford.

Emma, sipping her own drink, peered at the guy. She knew he was forty-three, two years her senior, but he looked wiry, as if he worked out. His thin, mobile features contrasted with a strong, square jaw. Black hair with a touch of gray at the temples made Crawford's silvery gray eyes even more arresting. *The portrait of a murderer?*

Cat continued in her throaty half-whisper, "Amazing that he scares women away. Even more amazing, instead of hating him, they adore him." She tugged Emma's elbow. "Come on. We'll say hello."

Emma had hoped simply to observe Crawford. "You know him?"

Cat chuckled. "As well as anyone. I've squeezed a couple of minute interviews from him before. I need another tonight."

After all, her college bud had procured her a ticket. Emma let Cat maneuver her between chatting people clumped together like flowers in an expensive bouquet. They worked their way across the large, exquisitely neutral room. If only Kelly could have accompanied them. Or Dottie Faye—

No. This time, her aunt might tackle Crawford. Thankfully, Emma and Kelly had managed to keep this party a secret, though Dottie Faye eventually would find out and remind Emma of her transgression *ad infinitum*. Dottie probably would have it chiseled onto her tombstone: "Died of a broken heart. Ask Emma why."

Cat strode toward Crawford, who was draped across an oddly molded chair. She dropped into a matching love seat across from him, pulling Emma beside her. "Hey, Kevin. Talk to me for sixty seconds, and I'll leave you alone the rest of the evening."

A tinge of a smile touched his lips. "I remember you. Subtlety's your strong point, right?"

"You *do* remember me." Cat wagged her head. "So's accurate reporting."

He gave Cat her minute. Then, without ceremony, she said, "This is my friend Emma Cotton, from near Boston. One of her relatives helps run the Berkshire Shakespeare Troupe in western Massachusetts—"

"Berkshire?" Crawford's face brightened as if she'd shone a spotlight on it.

Emma's stomach dropped to her stilettos. *Cat, what are you doing?*

Crawford fixed those marvelous eyes on Emma. "New York has Shakespeare in the Park during summer, but I would love to leave the city and take on some serious roles with Berkshire. They're one of the best."

Steaming, Emma turned to Cat, but saw only the wave of her hand as she mingled with the crowd.

Compared with this disaster, Dottie Faye's hot dog approach had been a stellar success.

Emma took a deep breath. "I don't know what possessed Cat, but I have no connections to Berkshire or any other Shakespeare company. I own a quilting shop and work in textiles, not theater."

She expected Crawford to invite her to take a hike out the eighth-story window.

Instead, a chandelier smile bounced light off every angle of his face, calculated to blind the viewer.

Wow. Now Emma knew why women ignored his moodiness. But why turn on the charm for *her*, the woman with zero connections to Berkshire or anything theatrical?

Crawford said, "Textiles have always interested me."

"Really?" *Most guys would never admit it.*

"I even took courses in college, though they had nothing to do with my major."

Yes, you took Rose's course. Emma swallowed. *The one she was teaching when she was murdered fifteen years ago.*

He'd also contributed to the signature quilt the class had made as a parting gift to Rose. Emma and Kelly had found this clue only recently, one that gave them the student roster the college had refused to provide. Crawford's blue and gold block, with his precise signature on the back, had been one of the better contributions.

"... I inherited an early twentieth-century Amish quilt. Vintage clothing from that era too."

Listen. Emma hoped she hadn't missed something important.

"My grandmother also passed down two small eighteenth-century Flemish tapestries to me."

Emma blinked. "You make it sound as if they were front-row seats to Knicks games."

"Well, I have those too." That smile again. "Just down the row from Spike Lee. But basketball aside, I do hope to build my textile collection. Do you restore quilts?"

Emma found herself chatting away. Surreal. Who would have thought she'd feel comfortable conversing with a possible murderer at a swanky New York gathering?

Though caught up in their talk, she noted he turned down waiters offering cocktails and hors d'oeuvres. Instead, Crawford munched on soy nuts from a muslin bag in his pocket and drank from his own stainless steel water bottle. *Why bring it to this upscale bash?*

Collecting DNA involved samples of hair, nails, saliva, mucus, or other bodily fluids, an especially tough task when dealing with a stranger. Tonight, the chances of collecting anything from Crawford appeared bleak.

She might snag samples, though, if she ran her fingers through that thick, wavy black hair.

This guy might be a killer! Emma shook herself. *What am I thinking?*

"What are you thinking, sweet pea?"

The familiar voice jolted Emma. She gaped at Dottie Faye, gorgeous in a black sheath with pearls Emma knew cost thousands. *How did you find out? How did you get in—?*

"Emma Jane, aren't you going to introduce me to this nice young fella?" Dottie Faye had morphed herself and her accent from hot dog vendor into Southern belle sophisticate.

Still numb, Emma complied. Before long, Dottie Faye's charm had extracted Crawford's deepest desire—to play Shakespeare's most challenging roles—and smoothly blended it into her strategy.

"I do *so* enjoy seeing young artists fulfill their potential," Dottie Faye cooed. "Are you doing *Hamlet* soon?"

"I … I'd love to." A muscle worked in the man's suddenly clenched jaw.

The longing that saturated Crawford's voice startled Emma. *So why don't you?*

Looking at his hands, he answered her unspoken question. "My agent says it's a matter of timing. My career's grown with lighter stuff, and I need to ride this horse while it carries me."

"Perhaps if you found someone willing to back your more serious endeavors, your agent might change his tune." Dottie Faye unleashed a toothpaste-ad smile.

His perfect mouth formed an *O*. So did Emma's. Dottie Faye, having baited her hook, steered the conversation toward his favorite spots in New York.

By evening's end, Crawford had invited Emma and Dottie Faye to a workshop the following morning. He handed them a brochure in which the director invited "our friends and supporters to further experience the theatrical world."

Translation: He caters to acting wannabes among VIPs who might donate big bucks.

Emma had to admit Dottie's party-crashing yielded excellent results. Plus, with a little maneuvering, she'd secured an additional invitation for Kelly.

Afterward, Dottie Faye insisted on sharing—and paying for—Emma and Cat's taxi. And though Cat had fibbed to Kevin and deserted Emma in her hour of need, her presence now delayed the first installments of Emma's penance a little longer.

two

"He's sick?" Emma stared at the young woman at The Paddington's workshop registration table.

"Mr. Crawford conveys his apologies. He woke up with a sore throat and must preserve his voice for tonight's show."

"We understand," Emma assured the girl, but she wanted to track him down and pound on his door. Was Crawford truly ill, or had he decided they weren't worth his time? Worse yet, had he somehow caught on to their real purpose?

"You're welcome to attend the workshop anyway." The girl handed them materials. "Mr. Crawford's understudy, Brett Damon, is excellent."

She turned to help other workshop participants. Emma, Kelly, and Dottie Faye huddled in an uncertain little group.

"He wouldn't get sick if he'd eat right. Soybeans." Dottie sniffed. "See what happens when you let all those health food hippies starve you with that stuff?"

Emma sighed. "What do we do now?"

"Let's go to the workshop." Kelly tugged on her arm. "How often can we attend a professional New York theater workshop for free?"

"Maybe I can teach *them* how to act." Daring kindled in Dottie Faye's eyes.

Kelly pulled Emma along before she could digest that comment.

The theater's dark red velvet curtain and old-fashioned brass sconces awakened inner magic. Even Dottie Faye kept quiet while the director, Connor Brannigan, ran actors through scenes from various musicals and one from *A Midsummer Night's Dream* to demonstrate blocking and timing principles. The actors shared with the audience how they met challenges they encountered.

Emma hadn't seen this musical version of Shakespeare's *A Midsummer Night's Dream* yet, but she'd attended the play. Brett Damon's exceptional portrayal of Puck kept her clapping well after he exited the stage.

The understudy actually resembled Crawford. Although Damon's features were more regular, his build, dark hair, and even some mannerisms reminded Emma of her new ... acquaintance. Her lips tightened. She certainly wouldn't call Crawford a friend.

Crash!

The attendees jumped. Amid a chorus of "What happened?" the director dashed backstage. He appeared a minute later. "A section of scenery fell. Caused a few minor injuries, but nothing serious, we hope—"

"I'm a doctor. I'll be glad to help." A distinguished-looking, bearded attendee stood.

"Thanks." Brannigan indicated a side entrance to the stage, and the doctor disappeared through it.

The director attempted a smile. "An unfortunate accident, but the show must go on, right?" He hurried actors out onto the stage, and before long, their antics had the group chuckling. The mood lightened more when workshop participants attempted the roles.

Even though—or probably because—Dottie Faye stood and waved her arms like a ship's signal officer, the director didn't choose her. Emma was thanking her lucky stars for his good sense when a stagehand approached Brannigan and whispered in his ear. The director abruptly announced a brief intermission and left with the stagehand.

"What's going on?" Dottie Faye echoed Emma's concern. "I hope no one was hurt worse than they thought."

A flutter unsettled Emma's stomach. "I'll find out."

She thought her aunt would insist on accompanying her, but Dottie Faye whipped out her pink phone. She began to play her favorite Civil War game, in which the Confederacy always won.

Emma hurried to the side aisle and slipped into the hall toward the stage exits so she could overhear the exchange.

"Mr. Brannigan, Brett and that doctor were right there, and then they disappeared!"

As urgent tones floated out the exit, Emma flattened herself against the wall.

"Skip the drama, OK?" Brannigan said.

Despite the circumstances, Emma almost grinned.

"Don't upset everyone," the director continued. "That doctor probably took Brett to the emergency room. Some doctors think they rule the world."

"But—"

"If anyone asks, tell them that." Heavy footsteps, as if Brannigan were pacing. "No one else was hurt. We'll finish this workshop and then track Brett down. Now, go and tell my assistant I need her. ASAP."

The stagehand rushed past Emma, who feigned distraction while she debated her next move. Despite Brannigan's blowing off of the man's concern, he had sounded worried. Emma crept closer and listened as Brannigan spoke into his cellphone.

"Privacy laws? Don't give me that. I'm a director. My lead is struggling with voice issues, and now my understudy went to an emergency room without anyone telling me. I have to put on a show tonight! Is he in your ER or not?"

Brannigan's side of the conversation disintegrated into

accusations and expletives, only to be replaced by a similar exchange after he hung up and called another hospital.

Emma stole back into the darkened theater to find her seat. As she sat, the director emerged and announced the program's final segment.

"Is everybody OK?" Dottie Faye's voice wasn't as quiet as Emma would have liked.

She whispered, "Apparently Brett Damon was the only one injured."

Kelly leaned toward Emma. "Badly?"

"They don't know. Gone to an ER."

Even the actors' excellent performance couldn't keep her focused. The minute the workshop adjourned, Emma jumped to her feet.

"Do you mind if we hang around the backstage area?" She pointed to the hallway where she'd eavesdropped.

"If you think that's important." Kelly searched her face.

"It might be. Or it might be nothing." Under Dottie Faye's scrutiny, Emma didn't want to say more. However, secrecy always brought out the worst in her aunt. "I'd like to know the details of Brett Damon's accident. I can't see any possible link between that and Rose's killer, but it just seems odd."

"Sure is." Dottie Faye patted her hair that she'd teased extra high. "So we're groupies? I can do that."

Emma winced. "Better that we simply act like who we are—workshop attendees."

"We don't want to stand out," Kelly added.

Dottie harrumphed. "You girls are no fun. But I'll be quiet."

Emma retraced her steps as the others followed, ducking stagehands who were hauling props to and from the stage. A muscular gray-haired man directed traffic.

"This looks so complicated!" Dottie Faye fluttered her

mascaraed eyelashes at the stage manager. "You're in charge of all this?"

The man's initial frown faded. "Yes, ma'am. A job that has to be done, but one nobody sees ... *if* you do it right."

"Sir, do I detect a teeny-tiny sound of the South in your accent?"

His eyes widened. "I was born and raised in Tallulah, Louisiana—"

"Just across the Mississippi from my hometown!" Dottie Faye clasped her hands. "I'm Dottie Faye Sinclair, originally from Vicksburg, and this is my niece, Emma Jane Cotton, and her friend Kelly Ann Grace."

"Jack Heaton." The man dipped his head. As they chatted, Jack occasionally tossed out directions to his crew. Emma exchanged smiles with Kelly. Her aunt could decimate an investigation, but sometimes she supplied exactly what was needed.

"Everything ran so smoothly today," Dottie Faye purred.

Emma and Kelly echoed her praise.

Jack dug his toe into the floor. "Well, most of it."

"I know you're *so* concerned about that boy who got hurt," Dottie Faye clicked her tongue.

The man's smile waned. "No way should that scenery have fallen. I check each backdrop before every show or workshop, then before every scene, to make sure the actors will be safe."

"I'm sure you do." Dottie Faye put a comforting hand on his arm. "Perhaps Brett ran into something in the dark."

The stage director shook his head. "No, Brett's a professional—doesn't stumble around in the dark or move stuff when he shouldn't." He raised his chin. "My crew didn't make a stupid mistake, either. Everything was as it was supposed to be."

"Is Brett in the hospital?" Although Dottie Faye could fool others when she chose, Emma knew her concern was genuine.

"Haven't heard anything yet. That was weird too." The man ran a hand through his hair. "I can't imagine Brett leaving without telling anyone. When we pulled that scenery off him, he'd taken a hit on the head. He was a little groggy, but he was conscious."

The flutter of disquiet now beat its wings against Emma's calm.

"Sounds like he'll be OK—especially since he received medical help so quickly." Kelly's ever-practical voice soothed the room.

Thanks, partner. Emma didn't want to rev up this guy and attract undue attention. She said, with her best smile, "We've never seen the backstage of a New York theater before. Do you think—?"

"Oh, Jack, I would *love* to see where you work." Another batted eyelash from Dottie Faye, and he ushered the women into the vast array of lights, backdrops, and ropes. Jack willingly answered their questions. Emma edged toward the back corners of the stage. A small space defined by curtains formed a break area with a coffeepot, chairs, and a dilapidated sofa that probably had served as a prop in its younger days. Behind the motley lounge, Emma noted a door with a red exit sign over it.

"Wish I could offer you coffee." Jack's dark eyes twinkled. "You wouldn't want that stuff. Only stagehands can drink it and survive."

"We really should go." Emma glanced at her aunt and Kelly. They thanked the stage manager effusively. Dottie Faye wished all her best to Jack's Aunt Minerva, who lived in the same Vicksburg senior community as Dottie Faye's Uncle Buddy Lee.

They returned to the front of the theater and blinked as they exited into noontime sun.

When they'd walked out of earshot, Kelly said, "OK, Emma, tell us everything you know."

She described what she'd overheard in the hallway.

"Brannigan's official version of Brett's incident makes the most sense," Kelly hedged. "But Jack didn't seem to agree."

"Actor types want to get on TV every time they have a nosebleed," Dottie Faye scoffed. "They don't try to hide something like this."

"Crawford wouldn't welcome the attention, but is Brett a recluse? I don't know." Emma threw her hands in the air. "I'm sorry he was hurt, and his disappearance was odd. But I can't think of a reason why this should bother me so much."

However, the next morning, when she read in Friday's *New York Times* that Brett's body was found floating in the Hudson River, Emma knew why.

three

"**I** am sorry." The tall, dark-haired woman guarding The Paddington's main entrance regarded Emma and Kelly with sorrowful gray eyes. "The theater is closed. Tonight's show has been cancelled in memory of Mr. Brett Damon, one of our actors, who died recently. I'm here to help with any ticket concerns—"

"No thank you." Emma let her own sadness flood her voice, adding the slight breathlessness of a groupie. "We thought Brett was a wonderful actor. We tried to see all his shows." She gestured toward the bouquet of flowers and bittersweet berries Kelly held. "We wanted to put these by his dressing room door."

"That's not possible." Though gentle, the woman's tone remained firm. She gestured toward other bouquets on a table. "I'll make sure his family sees them. You may leave a note, if you like."

She continued to eye Emma and Kelly as they wrote brief messages of sympathy.

No way will we slip past her. Emma had halfway expected the theater to be locked. This public relations lady's presence accomplished a similar effect, with no chance for Emma and Kelly to talk to anyone or uncover fresh clues.

For now, she'd have to siphon what she could from this spokesperson. "*The Times* didn't give many details. Have you heard anything?" Emma asked.

The woman stiffened. "The police instructed us not to answer any questions."

"We understand." Kelly eased the situation. "Thank you for your help."

"Thanks," Emma echoed, though she didn't feel appreciative.

"It was worth a try," Kelly said after they returned to the busy street. "We'll learn more Sunday night."

Crawford had called and invited them and Dottie Faye to have coffee with him after the show Sunday evening. Surely he'd heard more about Brett's killing than the police had made public. Hopefully the three women could eke out some details without putting Crawford on his guard ... though, for the hundredth time, Emma wondered why she couldn't leave this matter in the police's hands.

"We have to do this." Kelly was reading her mind, as usual.

"I know." When Brett had disappeared, Emma's gut had told her something far more terrible had happened than a bump on the head. Her instincts still refused to let her off the hook, though she continued to ask herself what this had to do with Rose's murder.

Emma swept her gaze down the street. "Why don't we walk to The Paddington's back exit? I can't imagine that the doctor could have taken Brett from the theater any other way."

"Too many people would have seen them," Kelly agreed.

As they turned the corner, Emma said, "Let's ask some of the workers in businesses across the street." She set her jaw. "*Somebody* had to have noticed something."

The wooden door they sought looked so ordinary. Only two days ago, Dottie Faye had set up her hot dog stand near it. The mental picture should have brought a smile to Emma's lips. But the door had proved a final exit for a life brimming with promise—a young, vibrant life ... like Rose's. A too-familiar burning seared Emma. She tried to quench her anger with a quiet assessment. "As far as we know, Crawford wasn't at the theater when Brett died. Nor can we prove he was present at Rose's murder—yet. But he's hovering in the background of both killings."

"So let's ask questions until we find out they're not connected." Kelly pointed to a nearby older hotel with black ironwork on its façade. A gray-haired, uniformed doorman surveyed the street as if it were his domain. "I'll bet he—or some other attendant—saw something."

Emma saw Kelly's gaze rotate to a woman dressing a mannequin in the store window next door. "Or maybe someone from the boutique."

"You just want to check out that mannequin's outfit." Emma had to smile. "But if we split up, we'll cover more ground. I'll speak to the doorman and then to the bellhops and valets. Then I'll ask workers at the café on the other side of the hotel."

"I'll take the two boutiques and the newsstand." As Kelly skittered off, she called over her shoulder, "Don't forget that Dottie Faye wants us to meet her cousin Lucinda for dinner tonight. Call me when you're done."

Emma gulped. She'd forgotten, a faux pas that would have precipitated a "hissy fit" as big as Dottie Faye's hair. Given their limited time to canvass the area, she'd better hurry too.

But she'd modify her strategy. The mention of Brett's death might put her subjects on the defensive. *The New York Times* had buried its brief account, treating the actor's demise as a "suspicious death," deep in this morning's pages. Perhaps some businesspeople hadn't yet read it or heard through the grapevine. As she crossed the street, Emma attempted to resume the adoring-fan expression she'd presented to the theater's PR lady.

"May I help you, ma'am?" The doorman dipped his head in a slight bow.

"I hope so." She held up the picture of Brett she'd printed

from his website. "Brett Damon's my very favorite actor, and I heard he was injured yesterday morning. Nobody will tell me if he's OK." She pointed across the street. "Did you see him carried out? Did an ambulance come?"

The man's courteous expression didn't change, but his voice tightened. "I'm sorry, but I don't recall anything unusual."

He touched his hat and turned to greet a guest who had driven his Lexus under the hotel's canopy.

Heat crept up Emma's cheeks as she returned to the sidewalk. *I wish I were a better actress.* Too bad Dottie Faye had scheduled a spa appointment today. She would have sold the groupie masquerade and charmed that doorman into telling what he knew. The guy probably noted every candy bar wrapper tossed onto his street. Emma refused to believe he'd miss a possible kidnapping.

Perhaps the doorman's boss had forbidden employees to discuss Brett, hoping silence might preserve the hotel's safe-neighborhood reputation. The doorman appeared to be just the man to enforce such a policy.

Pretending to peruse a menu posted outside the café, Emma watched a bellhop lug suitcases from the Lexus. A valet drove the car to a parking garage. Both appeared only slightly older than Kelly's son, Kevin. Maybe they'd talk more freely.

First, however, she'd check with the café employees. Maybe the doorman would take a break soon.

The only server in the nearly empty café was talking on her cellphone. Emma seated herself and waited. And waited. Finally, she rattled car keys on the table to draw the girl's attention.

With a deep sigh, the waitress hung up. She texted as she ambled toward Emma, stopping long enough to mouth, "Want a menu?"

With effort, Emma summoned a friendly smile. "No, just coffee, please."

Two calls later, the girl brought it. Emma pulled out Brett's photo and leaped into a conversation before the server could text again. "With the theater across the street, I bet you know lots of actors. Have you seen this man?"

She stared at the picture. "Maybe. I dunno."

Do you know what day it is? Oh, I guess you do, because that's on your phone. Emma made herself tell the server about Brett. She pointed toward the theater's exit. "Somebody said a doctor took him out that door, but I can't find out what happened to him. Did you see—?"

The girl's phone dinged with a text. Her eyes riveted to it.

Emma gave up, and the server wandered away.

The coffee surprised Emma. It tasted good. It was even hot. Apparently the phone addict functioned on autopilot. But Emma doubted she would notice a nuclear holocaust outside the café window. *Unless it shows up on her news feed.*

No employee could see The Paddington from the café's kitchen area, nestled in the back. If Emma returned tomorrow during the lunch or dinner hour, she might encounter a fully conscious server or cashier. Today, the hotel guys presented her best chances for clues. Emma gulped her coffee and left.

Good. The bellhop stood alone under the hotel canopy. Donning a distressed expression, Emma approached him. "Can you help me?"

As she showed him the photo and recited her Brett spiel, the young man's face mirrored her concern.

"I'm sorry about your friend. Yesterday before noon?" His sandy eyebrows crinkled. Then his face brightened. "I do remember seeing two guys—"

"Ryan, guests at the front desk need you." A sharp voice behind them straightened the boy's shoulders.

"But the lady asked me—"

"I'll handle this." The doorman's glare sent the bellhop inside. He turned to Emma. "I believe I answered your question earlier. I'm sure you understand that our first priority is taking care of our guests. I'm afraid neither I nor our bellhops have time to chat."

With difficulty, Emma held her temper. "I understand perfectly." She turned and strode away.

When she'd cooled down, Emma called Kelly, who also had finished her round of inquiries.

Kelly sputtered, "If the same thing happened in Mystic Harbor, my mother would have called the police, the medics, and the newspaper. She would have informed half the town by dinnertime."

"Nothing gets past Maeve." Emma's smile faded, however, as she thought of how little they'd accomplished. If only they could stay longer. But both had thrown on T-shirts and jeans before their unplanned venture to the Theater District. "We'd better go to the hotel and change, or Dottie Faye will have plenty to say about 'proper dress' tonight. Want to come back tomorrow?"

Kelly nodded. "Maybe I can sneak by the Nazi doorman and talk to the other guys. Or maybe he's off on weekends."

Her words were drowned out by a large food truck that roared by, turned, and parked on the street across from The Paddington's main entrance. Another followed it, sporting brilliant red, white, and green Italian flags and pictures of pasta on its sides. A smaller truck trailing, a potent fragrance of curry in its wake, pulled up and parked too.

Kelly sniffed and cast a longing eye in their direction. "Mmm."

"Kelly Grace, we're going to dinner." Even as she rolled her eyes at her friend's insatiable appetite, Emma wondered about the sudden influx of food trucks. *Of course.* Office employees who left work at five might grab a bite before going out. Also, the trucks probably were preparing for crowds who would attend the Theater District's Friday night shows.

Emma mused, "Thursday noon crowds probably don't attract nearly as many of these trucks as weekend performances. But maybe a few parked here yesterday near The Paddington. We need to ask around."

"A bunch of them will probably take advantage of the matinees tomorrow," Kelly said. "Let's aim for that."

As they rode the subway to their hotel, Emma wished she could stay at the hotel and do research. Fussing with makeup and clothes, going out—she wasn't in the mood. But they'd already read all they could about Brett and the killing. The New York City police reports on criminal cases weren't posted on the Internet. Even if Emma parked herself in front of the computer all evening, what could she do? Do an Internet search for "New York doctor"?

She sighed. Of course, she and Kelly would look for updates in the paper. She hoped that after tomorrow's round of questioning and Sunday's coffee date with Crawford, they would extract enough information to trace a faint outline of Brett's footsteps, now seemingly lost in the shadows.

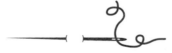

"Wow, where do we start?" Emma squinted at the food trucks parked near The Paddington. "French? Polish? Thai?"

"All of the above," Kelly said dreamily.

In answer to Emma's glance, Kelly crossed her arms. "I'll buy a few nibbles, but only to lower their guard."

"For investigative purposes only," Emma intoned, then grinned. "I might try a sample or two myself."

They'd entered the theater when the doors opened before

the Saturday matinee, only to meet the gaze of the PR dragon again. Two security officers were stationed in the lobby.

The hotel's doorman hadn't taken Saturday off, either. The phone-obsessed waitress and her fellow server appeared too busy to talk, so Emma and Kelly had decided to focus on the trucks.

They split up again. "I'll go left, and you go right." Emma gestured. "Meet you halfway around the block?"

"Gotcha." Kelly hurried toward the Italian truck they'd seen yesterday.

Emma approached one that served Filipino cuisine. The man at the counter pointed to a menu. "'Allo. You want spicee?"

"No thank you." When Emma showed him Brett's picture and asked if he'd seen the actor before, a wary expression stole the counterman's smile. He pointed to the menu again. "You want spicee or no?"

Did he think she was with the police? Emma fumbled her words. "He's a special friend. He got hurt Thursday morning, and someone took him away through that door." She pointed. "Were you parked here? Did you see him?"

The man frowned and persisted in thrusting the menu at her.

Though the counterpersons at the other trucks spoke better English, they shared the Filipino man's guardedness. Even a few who admitted they parked there on a regular basis said they hadn't seen or heard of Brett. Ever.

Emma didn't buy that. Dottie Faye had heard his name mentioned on the news last night. Though *The Times* included little additional information, the paper printed another blurb plus his obituary with a picture in Saturday's edition. *Somebody around here has to admit he existed.*

She spotted Kelly leaving a Polish truck. She was munching on pierogi, potato-stuffed dumplings. Emma said, "Any luck? Nobody on my end saw anything or anyone."

Kelly paused between pierogi and snorted. "Same here. I could swear one guy recognized Brett's picture. But it's like they all signed some sort of pact."

Emma shrugged. "I guess it shouldn't surprise us. I'd heard police in large cities often find it difficult to nail down witnesses."

They agreed to canvass the other trucks within a couple of blocks. Trudging through the Theater District, Emma's feet and hope grew colder with each negative answer. She saw a truck that advertised Middle Eastern food. The fragrance of freshly baked pita bread made her mouth water.

Why not? Kelly's probably eaten the equivalent of two dinners by now. Emma ordered a pita from a doe-eyed woman wearing a dark head covering. She spoke almost perfect English. When the woman handed Emma the steaming bread, she almost forgot to show Brett's picture. But she pulled it from her bag and asked if the woman had seen him.

The worker nodded. "Yes, he is a nice man. Always a smile. He likes pita bread too. But he looked ill when I saw him last."

Emma almost choked. "When was that?"

"Thursday, I believe. We heard that The Paddington was sponsoring an event." She frowned. "Before lunch hour, I saw a bearded man help that man"—she pointed to Emma's picture—"out of the theater's back door."

"Where did they go?" Emma's pulse thundered in her head.

"They entered a car parked nearby. The driver helped the sick man too. Did they take him to a hospital?"

The bread Emma had swallowed stuck halfway down. "I—I hope so. Do you remember anything about the car?"

"A dark-colored SUV. A late model." Instead of narrowing with suspicion, the woman's eyes widened. "You think they intended to harm him?"

"It's … possible. Do you recall what the driver looked like? or any other details?"

"Not really. I was watching your friend's face." Concern colored the vendor's tone. "I hope you find him soon."

"Thank you." Emma bid her goodbye and rounded a corner. She called Kelly and, in a low voice, told her about the conversation.

Kelly said, "Should we call the police?"

"Yes. Will you find a crime hotline number for me?"

Kelly didn't lecture Emma as usual about keeping up with technology. She called her back with the number a few minutes later. They agreed to continue scouring the area for additional witnesses.

Emma relayed the vendor's information, thankful for the hotline's confidentiality. But the few scraps she shared only fed her own determination to investigate this new mystery, as well as Rose's.

Emma watched theatergoers meander toward The Paddington for the afternoon performance before she trudged to the next block. At least they'd found one person who confirmed Brett's abduction. Next, they might visit the closest hospitals, though Emma doubted they'd learn any more than the theater's director had when Brett had disappeared. But even if they tracked him to an ER, how, within a few hours, did he go from the ER to the river? And why?

Was Kevin Crawford involved? His absence from the workshop appeared a little too convenient.

Like the pita, unanswered questions and obstacles stuck in Emma's craw.

No doubt, they were only the first of many questions impossible to swallow.

four

I may be the guest of a murderer tonight. Emma peered at herself in the hotel bathroom's ornate mirror, eyes narrowed, lips flattened in a grim line. Kevin Crawford might even be a murderer twice over. She had to consciously relax her mouth before she could apply lip gloss.

What New York visitor wouldn't dream of such a treat—sipping espresso with a star? Yet Emma could not dredge up her usual zest.

As she clasped her jade necklace, she pondered why Crawford would kill Brett—especially in such a public context. *Jealousy?* Crawford's popularity soared higher each week, so that seemed unlikely.

Did Brett have dirt on Crawford? Perhaps Brett had even stumbled onto clues that pointed to Crawford's involvement in Rose's death.

Get a grip, Emma. She fussed with her blond updo and yanked on gloves that set off her green silk dress. *Tonight you'll have to make nice.* Despite her gut reactions, she possessed only Crawford's quilt block from the class quilt and a witness's assertion that Crawford and Rose had argued the day before she died. No evidence at all connected him with Brett's death. But she would find out if it was just a coincidence.

If Kevin Crawford had killed either, he would not get away with it.

Kelly floated into the bathroom, a vision in amethyst tulle. "Girl, relax. Try to have a good time tonight."

"I feel more like attending a funeral." A video of Rose's sad service played in Emma's memory. "Let's go to Brett's wake tomorrow night. We'll learn more about him, maybe form a picture of why someone would want to kill him."

"Crash a wake?" Kelly's eyebrows rose. "I guess it makes sense. But tonight, let's focus on Kevin Crawford—and having fun."

"Kelly's right. No more talk about wakes and funerals." Dottie Faye, attired in gorgeous gold lamé, bustled into the bathroom, edging Emma against the wall and squishing Kelly's full skirt.

Emma's aunt dotted on a fake beauty mark, smiled into the mirror, and then turned back to them. "The secret to life, Emma Jane, is to make the most of every minute. We're feeling blue, but we're dressed to the nines, and we're going to have a ball at an off-Broadway play. We won't let sadness steal that from us."

Even as Dottie Faye spoke, Emma's chin lifted. Her aunt understood grief. She'd lost her husband, Archibald, in a tragic hunting accident less than two years after their marriage.

"The more we strut our stuff, the more we'll throw this Crawford fella off guard. So smile, honey." Dottie patted Emma's cheek. "Let's do it."

"Let's do it." Emma hugged her, and Kelly followed suit.

After a final glance in the mirror, Dottie Faye left the bathroom. Emma grabbed the glistening green, cream, and copper evening bag she'd sewn to match her dress. Kelly grabbed her embroidered violet bag, and Dottie Faye grabbed her favorite glittering gold purse with poofy silver roses.

Squished into a crowded elevator, Emma deep-breathed through her claustrophobia. While Dottie Faye conversed with everyone, Kelly murmured to Emma that they might strut their stuff to a lower degree than her aunt's aspiration.

"If she goes overboard," Emma whispered, "we'll initiate a primp break and hold her prisoner in the powder room."

"Gotcha." Kelly's eyes twinkled.

Emma still dreaded meeting Crawford after the show, but whatever ensued, it wouldn't be boring.

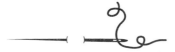

After a tribute to Brett with a moment of silence at the musical's beginning, The Paddington's production of *A Midsummer Night's Dream* proved even better than its reviews. The Greek lovers sang melting songs, the play-within-a-play actors had the audience in stitches, and the fairies appeared exotic, yet so real that Emma almost expected to encounter more around the hallway corners during intermission.

But she couldn't deny the obvious: Kevin Crawford as Puck outshone them all. The man who sat alone at the party had vanished. In his place, a wistful yet wild creature wreaked havoc with his mischief. When Puck attempted to help poor, spurned Helena, he sang a song about loneliness in a hypnotic baritone. Emma would never forget the pain in his voice, the power of those silver-gray eyes gleaming in his thin, striking face.

Emma shook off the magic.

The man was an actor. A very good one.

Emma noticed a lovely red-haired fairy in Queen Titania's entourage who cast a hostile glance at Puck. That didn't fit the story. *What's that all about?*

The play left Emma unsettled. She didn't want to knock at Crawford's door, but Dottie Faye wasn't shy.

He welcomed them into the scrupulously neat but cramped dressing room. "My friend Herbie made us coffee, and I had pastries brought in."

A skinny, bespectacled young man in jeans, perhaps still

a teen, grinned. "Kevin doesn't know beans about coffee, so I brew it for him when he has guests."

As Emma sipped, she debated how to approach Crawford. She couldn't look him in the eye, yet she couldn't stare at the aged hardwood floor.

Emma opted to talk to his nose. "The show was wonderful. You deserve the rave reviews you've received."

"He was great, wasn't he?" Herbie beamed. "Brannigan did a great job too, though he's shaken up."

Kelly chimed in her praise, and Dottie Faye flooded Crawford with a sugary river of accolades.

"Thanks," was all he said, but his nose and cheeks turned slightly pink.

Emma decided to go for the jugular. "You handled it amazingly well despite Brett Damon's death."

Silence. The nose paled.

"It's what we do." Crawford shifted his steel water bottle from hand to hand.

"Brett would have wanted the show to go on," said Herbie. From someone else, the phrase might have sounded trite, but Herbie's earnest tones made Emma think that yes, perhaps the young actor would have understood.

"He loved his work—he was so good that Dad talked about taking him on as a client." The boy's eyes teared behind his glasses. "I can't think of a single person who disliked Brett—and that's rare around theaters. Why would anyone want him dead?"

Nobody answered. Emma sighed. Nobody could.

Kelly, sitting closest to Herbie—and the exceptional croissants and canelés she'd likely spotted upon entering—patted his shoulder, her own eyes moistening. He gave her a startled but grateful look.

"Herbie knew Brett better than I did." A slight smile broke

out below Crawford's nose. "Herbie's on a first-name basis with everyone in theater."

Loud knocks on the door raised their heads. Herbie's tender expression hardened, and a muscle worked in Crawford's cheek. He answered the summons.

"Kevin, extra photo op in ten minutes. Outside, front of the theater." A tall, powerfully built man with mixed gray and caramel–colored hair pushed into the room.

"My agent, Reed Macklin." Crawford sounded as if he were introducing his least favorite teacher. "I have guests, Reed."

"It'll take fifteen minutes at the most." The man flashed a surprisingly charming smile. "You all understand, don't you?"

"Dad, give Kevin a break. Brett died only a few days ago." Herbie, much smaller than his father, stood toe-to-toe with him.

"It's OK, Herbie." Crawford touched the boy's arm and glanced at each of his visitors. For the first time, Emma matched his gaze. Colorless eyes met hers. The luminous power that mesmerized the audience earlier had vanished.

"Goodness, we all know Kevin has to sacrifice for his public." Dottie Faye rose to her full height, her magnet smile pulling another from the agent. "We're thrilled to have this opportunity to know him—and to meet you, sir."

Her model's stance exerted its desired effect.

"The pleasure is mine. We'll return in no time." Reed hustled Crawford out the door.

"Herbie, I'm sure Kevin appreciates all you do for him." With Kelly's tactful leap into the conversation, the boy's mortified expression eased.

"He's a wonderful performer. I try to be a friend to all the actors." He looked down at the floor. "Everybody, including my dad, wants something from them."

The honest devotion on Herbie's face made Emma's flush.

She hated being deceptive, even with a possible murderer. *But I'm doing the right thing too, Herbie. I'm Rose's forever friend.*

"I'm sure your father has good intentions." Kelly poured him a second cup of coffee. "After all, he's partly responsible for Kevin's success."

"I know." The young man rolled his eyes. "But Dad tries to bulldoze Kevin—and everybody else!"

It's the same with you, I imagine. The kid's upbringing probably differed radically from Emma's small-town background. Did he have a mother?

"It's a tough business." Kelly patted his shoulder again. "We're quilters, and even that makes me crazy sometimes. You deal with people, you expect stress."

She offered Herbie the last chocolate canelé. "Something this good always makes me feel better."

Her mom-like gesture brought back a vestige of a grin.

"Whoa, you really rate, Herbie!" Emma teased. "Kelly doesn't give up the last pastry to just anybody."

"Amen and amen," Dottie Faye looked at Kelly's small, trim figure. "Someday, I'm going to ask God why He designed her without fat cells and gave me an extra million."

"Um ... " Herbie closed his mouth.

Good job. Emma chuckled. *You're wise to leave that one alone.*

Kelly asked him more about the theater world, and he amazed them with his knowledge. Emma didn't look at Kelly, but she sensed their simultaneous *"Ding!"* Perhaps this young man could give them the inside perspective they lacked. Herbie already knew whom Brannigan had chosen as *A Midsummer Night's Dream's* new understudy. "Landon Green. He's good, but he's not Brett."

At the sight of Herbie's downturned mouth, Emma quickly asked him about the red-haired fairy who had given Crawford the evil eye—though Emma didn't put it that way.

Herbie knew whom she meant. "Madison Leigh."

Instantly, the sharp dark eyes behind his glasses softened, and the theater expert morphed into a lovesick teen. "She's really pretty—and a very good actress," he hastened to add.

"I'm sure she is." Dottie Faye gave Herbie her that's-so-sweet smile.

Kelly jumped in before he could take offense. "Is this her first role?"

"No, she's worked several shows. I really thought she should have played Titania. I know she expected it too." His face clouded. "Maybe it's just as well. She and Kevin don't get along. Once I overheard her blame him because she ended up without lines."

Before Emma could ask more questions, Crawford and Macklin returned. Kelly, whose son, Keith, was about Herbie's age, continued in her motherly role while Dottie Faye resumed where she'd left off in her efforts to fascinate the agent.

Emma realized her aunt had no serious designs on Macklin. She was cultivating the man's interest in case he might be useful, perhaps in providing clues about Crawford and maybe Brett's demise. His usefulness might even extend to unlocking the door to Dottie Faye's lifelong fantasy of becoming an actress.

Plus, she loved attention. Always.

Crawford dropped into his chair across from Emma.

"Mission accomplished?" She focused on his nose again.

He nodded and gulped from his water bottle. "I'm glad that's over."

Emma debated what to say. She'd already showered him with praise about his performance. What brilliant sentence would make him spill his guts?

She caught herself squinting because one of his nostrils was slightly bigger than the other.

"Have you been to the Roman Originals showroom?" asked Crawford, who had avoided the pastries, nibbling from his soy nut bag again.

Emma knew that name, one of the most innovative in textile design. "No. So far, Kelly and I mostly have hung out in the Garment District."

"It's several blocks away from the district per se, on Third Avenue," Crawford said, "but definitely a part of the scene. I used to go there often."

"I heard Roman designed 3-D textiles and mixed cloth with wood and rubber foam to create new fabrics." Emma found herself looking him in the eyes again, which now sparked with animation. "Though personally," she continued, "I prefer older fabrics. I don't foresee wooden quilts any time soon."

For the first time, he laughed stiffly, as if he had forgotten how. "I don't plan to add them to my collection, either. But I read that Roman also put together some nice historical exhibits in its showroom too, including quilts." A tinge of wistfulness colored his words. "If you and Kelly go, I'd enjoy showing you around."

Crawford had just offered a perfect opportunity for them to study him, possibly even collect DNA. Emma sucked in her breath and planed her tone to naturalness. "That sounds fun. I'll talk to her about it. Give me your number, and maybe we can work something out."

Oh, we'll work it out. Emma gave him her first genuine smile of the evening. *And you might be sorry we did.*

five

"I hope you're right about this." Kelly straightened her collar as they approached the funeral home.

Emma brushed off her coat. "Brett was an actor. Relatives expect a few fans to pay their respects." At the sight of the funeral home, though, she gulped. Small-town funeral parlors generally consisted of dignified old homes with porches and pots of flowers. Miller Mortuary, while tasteful, occupied a storefront. *The Godfather* sprang to mind, probably because of the large black hearse parked in front.

Suddenly, memories of their shop washed over Emma. Kelly's mother, Maeve, was tending Cotton & Grace in their absence, but Emma longed to watch sunbeams glisten on her spotless store window, to fold beautiful fabrics, to chat with longtime customers, her second family.

They entered and signed the guest register. Emma recognized three names, including Herbie Macklin's, his father Reed's large scrawl, and Crawford's precise signature. Her stomach lurched at the thought of facing him again, but he appeared to have come much earlier. She wouldn't have to talk to his nose again.

As she and Kelly entered the long, narrow room with its plush dove gray carpet and flowery fragrance, she saw Brett's portrait on a table beside a vase of red and white roses. Emma assumed the nearby silver urn contained his ashes.

She observed the diverse crowd. Men wearing dark sweaters and khakis mingled with Armani and Salvation Army suits. Girls with tattoos hugged grandmotherly types while women wearing pantsuits chatted quietly. A sprinkling of lively, dressed-up children dotted the dark landscape like sunbeams.

A wake is the oddest, most painful family reunion there is. Emma had breathed a sigh of relief when Dottie Faye's cousin Lucinda, who lived in an affluent Manhattan neighborhood, had tempted Dottie with a Fifth Avenue shopping trip and dinner out. This gathering didn't need another unknown factor.

A dark-haired woman and slim teen girl huddled near the urn—Brett's mother and sister, judging by the family resemblance. A large, blond man who occasionally tugged at his tie stood at their side. Should she and Kelly approach them? or simply mix with the crowd?

Kelly answered for her by joining others in line to speak with them. When their turn came, Kelly extended her hand. "I'm so sorry for your loss," she said kindly. "I didn't know Brett, but I saw him perform. His talent and vitality impressed me."

"He—he was excellent." Emma shook the woman's cold, dry hand. What else could she say?

"Thank you," the woman murmured. Those two words seemed to sap her hoarded energy.

However, they sparked the girl's dark eyes as if Kelly and Emma had demeaned Brett. "My brother was a wonderful actor and a wonderful person."

The blond man slipped an arm around the teen. "Anyone who knew Brett realized that, Leah."

His deep voice resonated with conviction equal to the girl's grief. Weeping, Leah buried her head in his shoulder.

"I'm Brett's pastor, Sam Dillinger." His compassionate eyes asked them to understand.

Kelly nodded her sympathy and walked back toward the entrance.

Emma paused. "Sir, where do you pastor?"

"Third Avenue Community Christian, near the Theater District." The big man's voice broke. "Brett was an active member. We'll miss him terribly."

Emma meant to follow up with Pastor Dillinger. He might know Brett better than anyone.

She wouldn't bother him now, of course. Emma followed Kelly toward the foyer in time to encounter Brannigan and other familiar faces from the workshop.

Herbie was right. The director's take-charge demeanor had drained away, leaving him limp and pasty. His eye fell on Emma and Kelly, as if trying to determine where he'd seen them.

"We were at the workshop Thursday morning," Emma said. "The morning Brett ...."

The man nodded violently, as if trying to stop her from saying the word. "I wish ...," he said.

Emma didn't need to hear the rest of the sentence. Brannigan wished he had checked on Brett earlier, wished he had taken his disappearance more seriously, wished he had followed his gut.

She knew what he was thinking because she had wished the same things ever since Rose died.

Brannigan ducked his head, a tear rolling down his cheek, and continued his path to the urn, the others following.

Emma's gaze returned to the portrait. *Why you, Brett?* His death didn't make sense.

Something was wrong both with this picture and with the smiling one by the urn that so resembled Kevin Crawford.

For the first time, a thought occurred to Emma. It left her airless.

What if Brett wasn't the actual target?

What if the murderer had wanted Crawford dead instead?

Pastor Sam Dillinger, standing behind a counter, wore a barista's apron that bore the Third Avenue Community Christian Church's logo. The minister gestured at the assortment of coffee flavorings behind him with a big, freckled hand. "What's your pleasure, ladies?"

My pleasure is ditching New York. Emma knew Kelly missed her husband, Patrick. In a few hours, the women would escape to Massachusetts on the New England Thruway.

Emma said, "I'll have a tall house coffee, thanks."

"Me too." For once, Kelly bypassed the tray of tempting muffins in the glass case.

"Nice and simple." The pastor handed them their drinks.

"If only life were like that." Even as Emma sipped the full-bodied brew, she knew returning to Mystic Harbor wouldn't help. They would pass the cemetery—and Rose's grave—on their way to the shop.

"Yes, 'simple' would be awesome. But I don't think it will happen. At least, not soon." A shrewd glint lit the pastor's gentle eyes. "Can I help you with anything else?"

"I think you can." Emma cast a quick look over her shoulder. In one corner of the church-owned coffee bar, a guy with dreadlocks stared, unblinking, at his phone; several older customers chatted over their drinks; and a young couple melded into a corner booth. "We don't want to intrude on your time."

"I'm due for a break." Pastor Dillinger served himself house coffee too. He gestured toward a bistro table at the empty end of the room. They sat, watching pedestrians wander past the window.

"I'm glad you're there for Brett's family, Reverend Dillinger," Kelly said.

"Sam." He grinned. "Reverend Dillinger is my grandfather." His smile faded. "Are you ladies Brett's friends? Relatives?"

"Neither." Emma lowered her voice. "We came to his wake because we hoped to learn more about him. You see, we are wondering if Brett's killer also murdered a close friend of ours."

They told him how Rose "accidentally" had fallen down the stairs outside her classroom fifteen years ago and how the local authorities had suppressed the DNA evidence under her fingernails to protect the college. Emma described how they had tracked a possible suspect to New York.

She ran a finger around her mug's rim. "I'm not sure if Crawford witnessed Rose's murder or actually killed her. But he likely could shed substantial light on her death."

"And you think he might have killed Brett?"

"Maybe." At this point, Emma didn't know what to think.

His eyes narrowed. "I assume there's another connection that makes you tie the two together?"

Emma fumbled her stirring stick. Kelly looked at her mug.

"I realize you don't want to make rash accusations," Sam said, "but if you suspect someone, you should go to the police."

"If we had a shred of evidence, we would." Emma bit her lip.

She thought about the evening after their funeral home visit, when she and Kelly had stayed up half the night, trying to puzzle out what they'd seen and heard. Then, for the past two days, they'd continued a fruitless search for witnesses around the Theater District. When tight-lipped ER personnel at nearby hospitals had stonewalled their questions, she and Kelly had begun a not-very-hopeful online scrutiny of medical staff pictures, seeking Brett's doctor.

"How can I help?"

Emma started from her reverie. Sam leaned forward on brawny arms, his green gaze riveted on them.

Kelly looked up. "You can tell us if Brett had any enemies."

"I don't know of any. Brett served in our church. He

spearheaded our program to help the homeless." A quiver started at a corner of Sam's mouth. He took a moment to steady his voice. "Brett and I were like brothers. If he'd struggled with a problem relationship, I think he would have told me."

Emma watched Kelly's eyes moisten. "I'm sorry," Kelly said. "I don't want to make this harder for you. But do you know any details about what caused his death?"

The pastor said nothing. His piercing gaze searched Kelly's face, then Emma's. As if satisfied, he said, "An overdose of ketamine, a sedative, killed Brett. The police told his family that no water was found in his lungs, so he was already dead before he was thrown into the river. Though the authorities still officially call it a 'suspicious death,' they're treating it as a homicide."

"Thanks." Kelly pressed, "Do you know if they have any leads on the doctor who disappeared with Brett?"

"If the police know something, they haven't shared it with the family. As far as we know, the guy seems to have disappeared into thin air." Sam spoke through gritted teeth.

"I'm wondering if he was an imposter. But doctor or not, whoever killed Brett obviously knew something about drugs." Emma probed further. "Did Brett have connections with anyone like that?"

"If you're asking if he used, Brett didn't." The pastor did not hesitate. "I knew him for more than seven years. I never saw evidence of that."

Remembering the actor's clean-cut persona, Emma didn't doubt it. Still, she had to ask. "Do you know if he had any history of drug abuse?"

"I'm sorry, but I don't discuss issues like that without a family's consent, and I won't ask for one. Not right now."

So Brett probably did use at one time. But what enemy from his past would kidnap him years later? And why such a public abduction? Emma wanted to hammer each question until an answer took shape, but when Kelly's hand squeezed hers gently under the table, she realized the big man had covered his eyes with one hand, his mouth working. Emma fell silent too.

Finally he spoke. "Whoever killed Brett may have stopped his heart, but the creep couldn't steal who he was." Sam wiped his eyes with the back of his hand. "Brett's with Jesus now, and he's making everyone smile, just as he did down here."

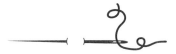

"Welcome home!" Maeve Quigley threw her arms around Kelly, then Emma. "Mystic Harbor couldn't stand one more day without you two."

"I think the town would survive." Kelly grinned.

"Your mother might not." Maeve hugged her again. "I hate to think of you girls in New York, riding subways with all those muggers."

"The shop looks great." Emma changed the subject. She loved the way Maeve folded fabrics exactly as she herself would have. She inhaled the shop's fragrance of lavender and lemon oil. Maeve must have polished the antique dressers that so beautifully set off quilts arranged in their open drawers. "Thanks for holding down the fort."

"My pleasure. How long can you stay?" Maeve's anxiety dissolved into a grin. "Dr. Hart wanted to know too."

Emma didn't want to think about leaving. She didn't want to think about Eric Hart, either. She should ask him about ketamine. But if Dottie Faye ever discovered Emma had contacted Eric—that "sweet-as-pie Southern gentleman"—in a nonmedical encounter, she would call their church about wedding dates. And order Emma's dress.

"We haven't decided when we'll return to New York." Emma rearranged the already-perfect folds of a lavender bouquet quilt. "When we do, Dottie Faye's cousin, Lucinda, invited us to stay with her for the duration."

"How nice. Maybe she'd like to keep Dottie permanently?"

"Mom!" Kelly eyed her reproachfully. "You should be ashamed of yourself."

"No, I shouldn't," Maeve said cheerfully as she took trash to the back door. "The Nimble Thimbles will accomplish twice as much at our next meeting without her big mouth. I don't think that woman's stopped to breathe since 1982."

Emma stuffed her belly laugh back down her throat. Dottie Faye couldn't stand Maeve, either. Often Emma and Kelly spent Nimble Thimble quilting sessions keeping the two women in separate corners. Perhaps this time, Emma and Kelly could focus on the group's project: a quilt featuring the seaside Mystic Harbor Pirate Museum.

The entrance bell announced Holly Locke, one of Kelly's favorite customers. A teen who preferred quilting to the Top 40, she sometimes attended Nimble Thimbles meetings. Emma left Holly to Kelly and headed for the storage room/office, stopping to finger knots on the colorful patchwork sun-and-sea hanging she'd made for the door. Emma entered to find Kelly's mother standing at the back exit, trash basket in hand, peering out its tiny window. "Spying on the neighbors, Maeve?"

She turned. No smile. "A man's loitering in our alley. That's the second time he's walked past. If he shows again, I'll call the police."

Emma cherished Maeve's protective bent, but she saw prowlers around every corner. "He's probably a tourist who's holding his map upside down. Stop worrying, Maeve."

Her friend grumbled, but she halted her vigil, updated Emma on the shop, and left for home.

Cotton & Grace remained open only a few hours more, but word spread of Emma and Kelly's return. Customers and friends welcomed them back. Marcia Goode, owner of Uncommon Threads, the sewing store whose upper story housed Nimble Thimbles meetings, asked Emma about Dottie Faye, who had stayed at her cousin's in New York.

"She won't be quilting with us this Saturday? What a shame." Marcia's pleasant Alabama drawl held nothing but sincerity. Still, her eyes twinkled. "Maeve will be so disappointed."

"I'm glad you're home." Walter Russell, a retired geometry teacher and the Nimble Thimbles' only male member, dropped by. "I hope you'll update us on your New York findings." He lowered his voice. "Please be careful, Emma. I support your desire for justice one hundred percent, but remember the fire that lawyer set here?"

I'm trying to forget. Imaginary mists attempted to persuade Emma that she smelled smoke again. She fingered the softness of an antique star quilt, hoping to convince herself that nothing would ever harm her shop again. "Don't worry, Walter. Kelly and I have each other's back, and Dottie Faye won't let anything happen to us. At least, not until she marries me off."

Walter grinned. "True." He listened as Emma described their adventures in the Garment District.

Most of the conversation centered on quilting. How she had missed everyday chitchat about the art she loved best.

Upon pulling up in front of her cottage, Emma wanted to give it a hug. The purple, pink, and white chrysanthemums on either side of her door had flourished during her absence under the care of her longtime neighbor, Edie Potts. She dragged her suitcase up the cobblestone walk, unlocked her door, and breathed in the air of home. It was, however, slightly stale, so she lit a pumpkin pie candle.

Even canned soup tastes better here. Emma ate while sitting before the gas fireplace in her grandmother's comfy antique rocker, feeling like a child again.

Staccato taps on the front door brought her back to the present. Sipping the last noodly spoonful, Emma rose and opened the door. Edie's little parchment face under her wooly hat crinkled into a huge smile.

"I knew you couldn't stay away much longer." Edie's black eyes sparkled.

"We're small-town girls, you and me," Emma said, never failing to marvel at the strength of the small woman's hugs. She invited her in. "Thanks for adopting my plants." Emma pointed to the philodendrons and ferns taking over her living room. "They like you better than me."

"Here's your mail." Edie handed her a paper bagful, then said abruptly, "I called Chief Kidwell and asked for an officer to check on your house from time to time."

Emma stared. "Why?"

"It may be nothing, but soon after you left, when I was cutting up firewood, I saw a man digging through your trash barrel."

"My trash?" How bizarre. Beeps resounded through Emma's mind like those that once preceded a dump truck's backup—before it crunched her Jeep.

"Of course, I said, 'What are you doing?'" Edie pursed her lips. "He didn't appreciate it."

"What were you thinking, Edie?" Emma winced at the mental picture of an attack on her friend. "He could have been dangerous."

"Pshaw." Edie crossed her arms. "I told him I'd call the

police if he didn't leave, then revved up my chain saw. He ran off with his tail between his legs."

Emma choked back a laugh, but her mind ran through a list of five-year-old bills she'd discarded earlier while cleaning out files. "Can you describe him?"

"Of course." Though in her seventies, Edie didn't need glasses. "Dark, scraggly ponytail and blue bloodshot eyes. Tall and skinny. Looked as if he hadn't seen soap in a long, long time."

A vagrant, looking for an intact piece of pizza. *Don't overreact.*

"He hasn't returned," Edie assured her. "If he does, I'll take my chain saw to that greasy ponytail of his."

"Um ... thank you."

Edie warned Emma to lock her doors and left.

Emma thawed a frozen apple dumpling, and after hesitating a moment, topped it with butter pecan ice cream. Eating at her kitchen table near the French doors, Emma ignored the glory of the evening sky's blossoming gilt clouds. Instead, her glances darted around her backyard, already cloaked in purple twilight. Did she detect movement over there? Or there? She considered installing a motion-based floodlight.

I'm letting my imagination run away with me. Stupid.

She fell onto the living room sofa. Her tired body embraced its softness.

But her mind refused to take the hint. It continued to run, its gears clinking and clashing like an oil-deprived engine. That night, Emma dreamed of Edie rampaging through Cotton & Grace, chasing the cast of *A Midsummer Night's Dream* with her chain saw while Emma downed plateful after plateful of apple dumplings.

SIX

"Ketamine?" Eric Hart's sandy eyebrows rose. "You don't need it, do you?"

"Of course not," Emma snapped, then relented. *It's not his fault the day fell apart.* Instead of catching a moment with him after his office hours, Emma had worked late. Eric, waiting for her at the shop, insisted on taking her to the Grounds for Suspicion Coffeehouse.

Dottie Faye's spies no doubt were videotaping their conversation.

Emma sighed. "I'm sorry. Too many things on my mind."

"Been there; done that." He smiled forgiveness. "Your aunt says you've encountered some complications."

Dottie Faye's probably sending you hourly emails. "I imagine she's told you about the actor found dead in the Hudson?"

Eric's grin faded to grim. "Yes. Do you really think his death is connected with Rose Peterson's?"

Emma looked him in the eye. "I don't know. But his proximity to a suspect in Rose's case makes me wonder." She enumerated on her fingers. "From all accounts, Brett Damon was well liked at work, active in his church, and concerned for the homeless. His pastor didn't know of any enemies who would kill him with a drug overdose." She leaned forward. "Would you tell me about ketamine?"

"Sure." Eric's professional persona emerged. "Ketamine's used as a sedative or anesthetic, especially in chronically depressed patients. Usually injected. Side effects include hallucinations or a pleasant dreamlike state. Not used much as a recreational drug, possibly because even a small overdose can be dangerous."

"In this case, it was fatal." Emma saw Brett's vital young face again as he acted at the workshop, his mother and sister's tears at the wake—too similar to Rose's wake fifteen years before. *I'll find these killers if it's the last thing I do.*

When Eric cleared his throat, Emma jumped.

"I hate to cut this short," the doctor said, "but if you have no more questions, I should go to the nursing home and check on Mrs. Whittington."

Heat crept up her face. "How inconsiderate of me. You're incredibly busy, and I've kept you from your patient." She gulped. "Thanks for talking with me."

"I'm glad to help any way I can." Sadness softened his wood-brown eyes, but his voice sharpened. "Be careful, Emma. I understand your concern, but if your suspicions are correct, you're dealing with criminals who will stop at nothing."

"I'm always careful." With Maeve fussing about loiterers and Edie waving her chain saw at trash pickers, Emma was growing tired of all the cautionary advice.

Eric insisted on paying for the lattes and left.

Sipping her now-cold drink, Emma reviewed their conversation. She hadn't expected Eric to react strongly to Brett's death, especially when losing patients was part of his everyday life.

Some people accused doctors of having no heart.

Obviously, Eric Hart was one doctor who lived up to his name.

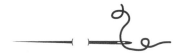

It's gone. Emma stared stupidly up the alley behind her shop. Down the alley ...

No sign of their trash barrel.

Don't jump to conclusions. Maeve probably told the garbage collectors to remove it, intending to purchase a new one. Emma, clutching a plastic bag stuffed with the remains of a gooey, impromptu Nimble Thimbles lunch, leaned against the doorway. *I don't need this.*

They couldn't continue their quest for Rose's killer without Maeve's help, but occasionally, she overstepped her bounds. Emma called to Kelly, who was carting bolts of material from the stockroom. "Do you know what happened to the trash barrel?"

"Why? Is it gone?" Kelly left the cart and poked her nose out the back exit. "Weird. It's not even trash day."

Kelly was right. Emma made herself ask. "Do you—do you think Maeve might know where it is?"

Kelly stared. "Why would my mother take our trash barrel?"

"Not 'take.' Maybe she intended to replace it with a nicer one."

"Yeah, she might do that, but I doubt she'd tote the smelly old thing off without telling us." Kelly's crinkled brows rose. "But I was the one who last emptied trash. I saw the old barrel last night. And Mom had a doctor's appointment in Boston today. She couldn't have removed it."

Emma smacked her forehead. "Even emptying the trash has turned into a major complication."

Beep, beep, beep. The mental alarm that had sounded when Edie told her about the trash picker now reverberated in Emma's head. "Kelly, we may have an identity thief on our hands."

Dropping the bag, Emma told her about Edie's incident. "We'd better check our credit card statements and bank accounts."

"Oh, no," Kelly moaned. She pulled out her phone and began tapping.

The bell over the front door jingled, and several smiling faces entered.

"I'll handle the customers," Emma whispered. "Just save our money!"

Kelly ran for the office. Emma shoved the bag into a corner and locked away her anxieties while she waited on tourists looking for Christmas gifts. Emma delighted them with handbags, praying silently all the while that no evil online wizards were devouring their resources.

She longed to dash to the office, but some customers who hadn't darkened the door in months wanted fabric and cutters. One even purchased a frame. Emma's phone dinged with texts, but nonstop business kept her from checking them. Finally the office door opened, and Kelly stuck her head out.

Smile, girl. Please! Emma waited for the thumbs-up that signaled their fears were groundless.

No smile.

As Kelly walked toward her, Emma wanted to sink through her cherished hardwood floor.

Instead, Kelly took over sales duties.

"I've done the business books. Check your personal accounts," she whispered.

Emma hurried to the office, yanked credit cards from her billfold, and scrolled through her online statement. Huge balance, but she'd expected that after their stay in New York and because she hadn't yet paid her bill this month.

Hotel ... restaurants ... theater tickets. And a four-thousand-dollar charge at a casino in Nevada last night. Emma sucked air, but found no oxygen.

Her fingers fumbled at keys as she tried to bring up her bank statement.

A seven-thousand-dollar withdrawal. Yesterday.

Emma sank her heavy head into her arms.

Kelly's voice. Her warm arms surrounded Emma's taut shoulders, and her cheek rested against Emma's icy one. "We'll weather this, Emma. What's your credit card company's number? There's our bank number, since we use the same one. I already called the police."

Mechanically, Emma made calls, spoke with sympathetic disembodied voices, answered questions.

Why, oh why didn't we buy a shredder? Even as Emma reproached herself, she knew why. Neither she nor Kelly thought they would need one in Mystic Harbor, Massachusetts.

Tom Boyer, now deputy chief of Mystic Harbor's police department, stopped by and asked more questions. The last time she'd tried to convince him that Rose's fall down the stairs was not an accident, he'd stared at his computer screen, his phone, the floor. Now, as they discussed the theft in the shop's office, he looked Emma and Kelly in the eyes.

Emma told him Edie could give a description of the trash picker. Boyer said he would talk to Maeve about the loiterer too.

By then, both Emma and Kelly had surveyed the financial damage. When Emma added up all her unauthorized personal debits and purchases, they totaled $11,972.33.

Kelly's added up to $7,449.81. "Yes, he found my trash barrel too."

"I'm sorry you two have suffered such big losses." Boyer shook his head as he made notes on his phone. "I've already talked to the FBI. We'll do everything we can to find this guy."

The thief had stolen more than fifteen thousand dollars from their business accounts and charged another three thousand on the company credit card.

"Only three thousand? He stole more from my private account. Not very efficient of him." Emma tried, unsuccessfully, to drag a smile out of hiding. "After all, our business account has a much higher limit."

Kelly, so calm during the past difficult hours, now sparked with anger. "We'll make him sorry he ever thought of taking our money. We'll hand him over to the Nimble Thimbles."

"Let's give him to Dottie Faye. She'll sit on him and rat his hair with a comb until he screams."

At last, Emma coaxed a small giggle from her stone throat. Kelly laughed too. Neither came near breaking the belly buster barrier, but even a hint of mirth tasted good.

Boyer's eyes widened as he looked from Kelly to Emma. Their giggles grew.

You can't break us, Emma thought defiantly, then stopped short. Was he just a common, contemptible identity thief? Or did a larger scheme hide behind his larceny?

"This guy wants us to give up on finding Rose's killer," Emma said softly through gritted teeth. "He wants to beat us down and make us quit."

"Fat chance." Kelly crossed her arms.

Boyer frowned and looked away, as he always did when someone mentioned Rose. "That's quite a leap—from a death fifteen years ago to online theft now."

Emma saw worry clouding his eyes. But nothing they could say budged Boyer. He was convinced there could be no possible connection between the crimes.

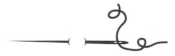

That Saturday, the Nimble Thimbles unanimously affirmed Emma and Kelly's hypothesis. Marcia Goode, Tokala Abrams, Walter Russell, and Holly Locke already had heard about the theft in the newspaper. As they pieced together the Pirate Museum quilt, the sunlit upper story of Marcia's store buzzed with indignation.

"Any idiot could see it," Maeve fumed. Eyes ablaze with green fire, she stabbed her needle through cloth and batting. "Has this criminal targeted anyone else in town?"

"No!" the other quilters chorused.

"First this creep murders my girls' best friend, then he cleans out their money!" Maeve waved her shears at the invisible enemy. The quilters answered with a growl of fury.

Emma decided she'd better calm them, or this Nimble Thimbles vigilante committee might riot.

"Thanks for your love and support." Warm tears welled in Emma's eyes as she ducked Maeve's shears to join Kelly in hugging her mother. "Our lawyer is talking to our bank and the companies involved to try to work this out."

"I should hope so." Marcia squeezed Emma and Kelly's hands. "This is unacceptable." Her eyes flashed. "Completely unacceptable."

Walter, his kind face empathetic, patted Emma's shoulder. "If you need financial help—"

"We'll be fine," Emma reassured him. Down through the years, she and Kelly had squirreled away a joint emergency fund at a different bank. Because the account remained largely inactive, the thief must have found nothing in their trash that betrayed its existence.

It might keep them afloat until the holiday season replenished their coffers. But Cotton & Grace would have to stay open morning, noon, and night, despite trips to New York.

Maeve read their minds. "I'll work as long as you need me."

But Maeve couldn't spend 24/7 at the shop.

"While you're away, I could help out two nights a week." Tokala's lovely dark face glowed with concern.

"I could work an evening or Saturday each week," Holly offered.

Walter and Marcia chimed in, and Emma's gratitude filled her throat so she couldn't speak. Biting her quivering lip, Kelly said, "Thank you all. We won't be able to pay much—"

"Who said anything about pay?" Tokala demanded. "You've taught me so much over the years."

At the chorus of agreement, Emma and Kelly couldn't hold back the tears. Finally, Emma stuttered, "We—we're not making much progress on this quilt today."

Kelly dabbed her eyes. "Remember, the city will want to raffle it off at the spring festival. May's coming faster than we realize."

Marcia picked up her needle. "Let's move it, quilters."

For the next two hours, they cut and stitched in a blur. Emma poured herself into sewing quilt blocks as if they would help her piece together the clues to Rose's death. To Brett's death. And to Kevin Crawford's role—if any—in both.

At session's end, Marcia beamed. "Go, Thimbles! We completed even more than usual."

They tidied the studio and celebrated with turtle brownies at the Chocolate Cauldron Bakery.

Only after Emma and Kelly returned to Cotton & Grace did Emma find the sizeable check Walter had tucked into her sewing apron pocket.

"For Rose," he'd written on an accompanying note, "and for Brett, two young people whose lives should have been longer."

Wordlessly, Emma showed Kelly the check. They clung together in a silent pact that nothing would keep them from ferreting out the truth.

Nothing.

seven

"Whoa, am I glad you guys are back." Herbie Macklin hugged Emma and Kelly as if they were long-lost relatives.

Emma exchanged quizzical glances with Kelly. They hadn't seen Dottie Faye yet or her cousin, Lucinda, though they'd talked on the phone. They hadn't even finished unpacking their bags in Lucinda's gorgeous guest rooms when Herbie had called Kelly on her cell, then had arrived on the doorstep. Now they relaxed in the three-season room, enjoying hot cider.

Emma lay back in a cushy chair, breathing in the faint but spicy fragrance of the many-colored potted chrysanthemums and marigolds. "Boy, does this beat fighting traffic."

"You drove?" Herbie eyed her as if she'd ridden in a buggy. "When Dottie Faye told Dad you were returning to New York, I thought you'd take the train or fly."

"I like driving my Jeep." No need to reveal her terror of flying.

"Anyway, I'm glad you're here." Herbie's smile widened for a moment, then faded. "Things got weird around The Paddington while you were gone."

Oh, goody. More weirdness. Emma tried to keep her expression neutral. She and Kelly had agreed not to discuss the identity theft with anyone.

"What kinds of things?" Kelly leaned forward.

"Nothing big." Herbie frowned. "Some of Kevin's stuff has gone missing during performances. Last night, somebody removed a costume from his dressing room. The dresser swears she left it where she always does. So he had to wear one that didn't fit. Also, the fake love-in-idleness flower—you know, the magic flower in the musical that makes the characters fall in love—disappeared."

And? Emma waited to hear more. Surely this type of thing happened occasionally, even in off-Broadway productions. After the past week of police interviews, credit card and bank account changes, and phantom stalkers who haunted her footsteps, a misplaced costume and missing flower seemed inconsequential.

"Kevin couldn't handle it. He freaked offstage, but a prop guy calmed him by borrowing a flower from a bouquet some-body's boyfriend had sent. Kevin did his usual fantastic job, though his tights bagged at the knees." Herbie grinned sheep-ishly. "I know all this sounds dumb. But it shook Kevin up."

"So Kevin doesn't usually react that way." Kelly leaned on her arms.

"He's an actor. All of them get weird. It's part of the job description." He shrugged. "But Brett's death has really messed with his head."

Kelly tried to help the boy focus, but he couldn't nail down what troubled him about Kevin.

Not for a moment, though, did Emma discount his concern. Herbie knew Kevin better than anyone else at The Paddington.

The brilliant, introverted actor was struggling. With what?

Guilt over masterminding Brett or Rose's death—or both? Remorse for concealing evidence?

Or did Kevin fear for his own life, conscious that someone intended to murder him and had killed Brett instead? Perhaps it was the woman whose DNA was found under Rose's finger-nails? Maybe she had decided to eliminate Kevin, who could implicate her in the crime.

Welcome back. Emma smiled wryly as clueless Herbie happily updated them on other theatrical gossip. The "rest" in

Mystic Harbor hadn't cleared their heads. They'd have to force tired brain cells to deal with problems that had only festered in their absence.

When the teen paused for breath, she asked, "Does anyone at The Paddington know that doctor who attended the workshop?"

Herbie shook his head. "I heard Ophelia—she's Brannigan's assistant—talking to him about it." He intoned in a deep voice, "She sees and knows all."

"Tall, dark woman?" Kelly asked.

"The take-charge type?" Emma prompted. *Ophelia—the perfect name for the PR dragon who guarded the theater after Brett died.*

"That's her." Herbie nodded. "She said she wasn't aware any doctors had signed up, though they don't always use 'Doctor' in their registrations. But she was sure of one thing. She told the cops no bearded guys came to that workshop."

"So whether wearing a real beard or disguise, the man who 'helped' Brett had sneaked into the workshop." Emma exchanged triumphant glances with Kelly. "Not very doctorly of him."

Herbie snorted. "Sometimes people you wouldn't expect act like little kids. Once a CEO who wasn't invited crashed a workshop because Brannigan invited one of his competitors."

He chattered on about other strange attendees. When the teen showed no signs of leaving, Emma and Kelly combined diplomatic forces to edge him out the door.

The moment Emma shut it, Kelly blurted, "So what do you think about the doctor?"

"If not a fake, the guy obviously was hiding something," Emma said grimly.

They decided they'd keep searching hospital staff pictures for him, but they wouldn't make it their top priority.

As they finished unpacking, Emma pondered Herbie's visit. She and Kelly would need every ally they could muster to untangle the snarled threads of these impossible cases. Though Herbie pursued them like a yappy, too-eager puppy, this see-all-know-all teen might prove invaluable.

"Do you have enough for your day on the town?" Dottie Faye's voice halted Emma and Kelly as they were about to exit the grand foyer of Lucinda's townhouse.

Blast. She knows. Emma turned and tried to inject a teasing note into her voice. "Do we have enough what? Pepper spray?"

"Coupons?" Kelly joked.

"Nice try, girls." Dottie wagged a finger, her poofy 'do mimicking its movements. "I know all about that terrible person stealing your money. Why didn't you tell me?"

Emma heard more than a hint of hurt in her tone. She clasped her aunt's hand. "I'm sorry. We didn't want to worry you."

Dottie Faye trumpeted, "And it doesn't worry me when I overhear some lowlife has robbed my only niece?"

Emma dropped her gaze, stealing a glance at Kelly, who had dipped her head too. Emma mumbled, "You're right, Dottie Faye."

"We're sorry," Kelly ventured. "But we knew you would want to help—"

"What's wrong with helping you a little?" Dottie stabbed her hips with candy-pink nails. "That's why the good Lord gave me all this money."

Emma protested, "But you've helped us so much already."

"And I'm going to keep helping you until we catch this …

this scum who killed Rose and that nice young actor. Is that a crime?" A vein in Dottie's forehead throbbed.

Lucinda, a plumper, darker, and quieter version of her cousin, glided into the foyer. "Dottie Faye, honey, the girls didn't want to upset you. They know it's bad for your blood pressure."

Emma waffled with her thoughts and words. *Don't promise to tell her everything.* "We'll try to keep you on top of things from now on."

"Honest." Kelly nodded, six-year-old style.

"Well, OK." Dottie Faye wilted. Fine wrinkles around her mouth deepened so that momentarily, she looked her age. "I forgive you."

They hugged her, and Emma thought about her father, living in far-off Florida, about her late mother's arms around her—and how she valued Dottie Faye's.

"Now please answer my question." Dottie Faye drew back and eyed them sternly. "Do you girls have enough money?"

"Yes." Emma told her about the emergency fund and Walter's gift.

"Walter's a nice man." Dottie wiped away a tear. "If he wasn't a Yankee, I might ask him to tea."

"Reed's a Yankee too, Dottie Faye." Teasing lit Lucinda's violet eyes. "But you're going to lunch with him."

"That's different, and you know it." Nevertheless, Dottie Faye moved within range of a magnificent marble-edged mirror and smoothed her hair. "The girls and I are gathering information about Kevin Crawford. Who knows him better than his agent?"

"If you say so, dear." Lucinda patted her shoulder with a small, wicked smile and left.

"I appreciate what you're doing, Dottie Faye. I'm not sure

I could bear an afternoon with Reed." Emma frowned as she recalled how the agent had coerced Kevin and upset Herbie.

"Everything's all about him," Dottie agreed cheerfully. "If I stay sweet, ask the right questions, and let him talk his head off, I'll learn a lot."

"He strikes me as the perfect criminal personality." Kelly wrinkled her nose.

"Too bad he's not a suspect," Emma agreed. "Herbie said his dad was thinking of signing Brett as a client. Kevin brings in big bucks—no motive to kill him off, either." Emma clicked her tongue in mock regret. "Reed wouldn't do in the goose that lays the golden eggs."

Dottie Faye, immersed in the mirror, did not seem to hear. She flashed it a final smile, then turned, à la New York runway, to face Emma and Kelly again. "Let's touch base when I return, shall we?"

Before they could respond, Dottie Faye said, "I'm so glad we've worked out this silly business of keeping secrets from me." Her potent blue-eyed stare returned. "You may fool other folks, but as far as I'm concerned, Emma Jane and Kelly Ann, you're the world's worst liars."

With that, Dottie Faye flounced out of the foyer.

"Whew." Kelly stared after her. "At first, she sounded almost as mad as when you and I entered that mud wrestling tournament."

"The only reason she didn't disown us was because we did it for charity." Emma chuckled. "In her mind, we'll never learn to act like ladies."

Kelly grinned. "We're hopeless."

"I think she had a point this time. We didn't just leave her out of the loop. She felt left out of the family." Emma bit her lip. "Let's not do that again." The enormous grandfather clock in the foyer began to bong.

"Ten o'clock." Emma grabbed the bag she'd dropped and opened the door. "Ack! We're supposed to meet Kevin at the Roman showroom at eleven."

They hurried to the nearest subway station, Emma wishing she could drive to her destinations in ten minutes, as she did back home. Instead, they rode escalators and pushed, with thousands of other people, through doors of trains that *clack-clacked* along tracks under the city. Everyone moved as if by remote control, unnerving after friendly Mystic Harbor. But a dozen languages floated around Emma as she clung to the trains' shiny poles. She loved the varying textures of the city landscapes, the champion pace of lights and buildings rushing past the windows.

She didn't, however, like the nagging feeling that she'd fought in Mystic Harbor since the identity thefts, the continued sense that someone was following her.

Of course people are following you. They're going to the 59th Street station too.

She and Kelly exited, shivering as they walked to Third Avenue and the venerable brick building that housed the Roman Originals Textiles showroom. As in other buildings, the plain front reflected nothing of the elegance within. The designer had blended brick walls and sleek bronze decor with glistening earth-toned banners hung in layers from the ceiling, accented by strips of silvery turquoise. Several people, carrying briefcases and talking on phones, hurried to elevators, but Emma stopped to inhale the scene, ignoring the certainty she would be labeled a tourist.

Kelly halted too. "Love it," she murmured.

Emma nodded. And this was only the entry!

She glanced at her watch. Still fifteen minutes before Kevin was to meet them. She and Kelly should review the day's plan.

"How does this sound? We try to lead Kevin back to his college days and draw him out about Rose ..."

"And find some way to collect his DNA," Kelly finished. "He'll probably bring that blasted water bottle."

"I hope he doesn't bring his lunch." Emma pondered the possibilities. "I have it. You hide behind a display, mug him, and steal his water bottle."

"Why me?" Kelly objected. "You clobber him and yank his hair out."

"Easy, right?" Emma grinned ruefully. "I wish."

"Maybe we can talk Kevin into lunch out."

"Or a snack break," Emma sighed. "We'll have to stay on DNA alert all day." She patted her bag. "I brought envelopes in case we get lucky."

Eric Hart had told her the plastic bags she saw on television could damage DNA samples. She should write him a thank-you note for all his help. If only Dottie Faye wouldn't jump on that, as she herself would say, like a chicken on a June bug!

A warm baritone "Hey!" sounded from the other end of the room. Emma glanced at Kelly, and they began their tour of the delightful textile showroom with a man who might be a killer.

eight

"Welcome back." Crawford's chandelier smile glowed.

A twinge of guilt, like a toothache's onset, niggled at Emma. And yes—she sighed—his steel water bottle hung from his belt. "We're glad you could make it."

They exchanged a few pleasantries. His smile faded when they asked him about the musical, but it returned quickly as he glanced around the high-ceilinged room. "I've wanted to do this since forever." He led the way to the elevator.

New York boasted way too many of them. Emma grabbed the brass rail that lined its walls. *At least it's not a glass elevator.*

"When did you become interested in textiles, Kevin?" Kelly's voice calmed Emma as they rode to the fifth floor.

"I can tell you exactly when it happened." He flashed another smile. "When I was a child, Grandmère Henriette let me touch the two Flemish tapestries she eventually passed down to me. I had to be very careful because they were quite old." He shook his head. "I couldn't believe weaving threads together could make something that beautiful."

The elevator stopped, and Emma edged toward the doors. Being trapped in a small space with Crawford unnerved her, even if he had a sweet Grandmère Henriette.

But her misgivings untwisted as she stepped onto Roman Originals' polished chocolate brown granite floor and wandered the company's displays. Waterfalls of colorful cloth spurted from stone walls. Bronze grids stored folded fabrics and quilt patterns. Spiraled fabric sculptures containing bamboo, wood, and precious metals adorned the room's corners. Long work tables with sleek bronze lights invited patrons to examine Roman offerings more closely.

Nosing around fabric like a curious Irish setter, Crawford in no way resembled a criminal. Nor did he display the emotional instability Herbie had described. Perhaps the teen was projecting his own struggles with Brett's death onto Crawford.

Emma and Kelly found themselves discussing cloth with the man as if he were a member of the Nimble Thimbles. Roman Originals touted solids and elegant geometric patterns. Innovative textures dominated here, with random piles and patterns. Roman also introduced new eco-blends of cloth, including pinewood, algae, soy, and stinging nettles. Emma gathered samples for her fabric book. She could visualize them in handbags, and some of her wealthier or trendier customers might enjoy their novel fiber content in quilts. But most shoppers in Mystic Harbor preferred to pay less for more traditional materials.

You're acting as if this is a purchasing trip, Emma castigated herself. *Get him talking about Rose.*

"Kevin," she said, "you mentioned that you took college courses in textiles. Where did you go to school?"

"In your backyard. Hawthorne College, just outside Mystic Harbor."

"We both went to school there! Why didn't we see you?" Kelly sounded so innocent that Emma fought a grin.

"I was a late starter." Crawford shook his head. "I fried burgers several years before I realized I wanted to do more with my life. I went back to school, though I never was good at academics." He fingered a large terra-cotta sculpture that bowed and undulated.

"I majored in art as an undergrad and took the few textile

courses they offered," Emma said, "but I heard Hawthorne really expanded its curriculum after Kelly and I graduated."

Crawford shrugged. "I liked Hawthorne, but I've probably learned more by digging on my own—not because of the profs or courses, but because of me." He grinned. "I took that approach to theater too, and just about everything else. If I turn my work into a hobby, I work much harder at it."

It was an interesting discussion, but this wasn't taking them any closer to Rose. How Emma wished she could yell "Rose Peterson!" and see how he reacted.

Kelly seemed to sense her impatience and threw Emma a warning glance.

Emma shot back one of her own. *Chill, Kelly. You know I won't blow it.*

Emma only half-listened to Crawford as they returned to the elevator, but she noticed for the first time that he sounded snuffly.

Eww. She braced herself. Emma didn't like to think of grabbing used tissues, a possible transmitter of DNA. But if she could, she would.

"Blasted allergies." He paused before honking like a congested goose, but he used a spotless white cotton hand- kerchief. It looked freshly ironed. Herbie had never mentioned a woman in Crawford's life. Maybe he lived with his mother? Did he *iron* his handkerchiefs?

Emma knew this shouldn't freak her out; she loved fabric and rejoiced to see it used rather than disposables.

But this was just weird. Maybe Herbie *should* worry about Crawford.

The next floor brought them to A. Roman Furniture and Carpets. "Are we interested?" Kelly asked, her hand poised over the button panel.

They decided to take a quick look. Both Emma and Crawford liked one plush sofa embroidered with brilliant strands of color reminiscent of his tapestries, and Kelly exclaimed over a stained glass patterned rug. "Can we take the stairs to the historical floor?" Emma proposed. "I need exercise." The others agreed. Instead of the elevator feeling, however, the feeling of being stalked accompanied Emma as their footsteps echoed in the aged, bare brick stairwell.

Too many mysteries on the nightstand, Emma. She ignored the events of the past two weeks, hammered a plug into her gushing imagination, and aimed her gaze upward.

The historical display didn't fit Roman Originals' style, so the company had not developed it as much, though Emma appreciated the bow to the past. The exhibits included a nineteenth-century display of clothing that ranged from hardy pioneer linsey-woolseys and denims to opulent Gay Nineties ball gowns and tailcoats with white ties.

"Not Shakespeare costumes, but interesting. Once I endured a tie like that in a college production of *Hedda Gabler.*" Crawford made a gagging motion. "Even worse than wearing tights."

Wandering into the next niche of the display, Emma drew a breath of delight. After all the trendy fabrics and furniture, a small home away from home greeted them. Glass cases preserved antique quilts of various sizes that shared their colors and their stories.

"Yes!" Kelly apparently felt the same way.

A pre-Civil War group of Quaker women had sewn prayers and poems into one quilt's quiet gray, brown, and cream-colored folds, every day whispering defiance against slavery. A faded but bravely colorful crazy quilt sewn by nineteenth-century pioneer women, plush velvet quilts from an industrialist's mansion, and a Depression-era baby quilt made from flowered feed sack material all made Emma's fingers itch to grab a needle. That was the problem with museums—she couldn't touch the fabric!

"Want to find a frame somewhere?" Kelly spoke beside her. "There has to be a quilting group around here."

Emma grinned ruefully. "I doubt Lucinda's friends are into sewing." She and Kelly had brought bags of blocks to embroider, but those fun, heart-to-heart Nimble Thimbles sessions in Marcia's quilting studio made her heart sing.

"I started a Shakespeare quilt."

At Kevin's voice, Emma jerked. Just when she forgot his existence, he turned up again.

Kelly chimed, "I didn't know you quilted, Kevin. How did you learn?"

Of course. Emma almost slapped her hand aside her head. *Get him talking about quilting. Steer him toward Rose's class.* Surely he would describe the well-designed dark blue and gold block he'd made for the class quilt.

Instead, he mentioned his grandmother again. "Grandmère showed me the basics. I made a small Boston Celtics quilt when I was eleven." With a conspiratorial grin, he lowered his voice. "Don't tell Spike Lee. OK?"

Emma laughed. "In one course I took, we each designed and contributed a block to a class quilt. Did you?"

"I don't remember." He shrugged, and then the smile returned. "Good thing I'm better at memorizing Shakespeare than remembering college stuff, right?" Determination gleamed in his eyes. "At the present rate, I'll work on my Shakespeare quilt the rest of my life, but I'll finish it. I'm portraying plays I've done, so now I'm working on the *Midsummer Night's Dream* block—a purple flower and the magic drops of nectar that, you know, spread the love around."

Kelly asked more questions about his design, but Emma

could only fume, though she smiled and nodded at what she hoped were appropriate moments. When it came to meandering past real issues, the man was an absolute genius.

He's an actor, Emma. Remember that.

Good thing one part of her brain had stayed awake. She personally struggled with deceiving anyone, but this guy's whole job consisted of fooling people.

He probably enjoyed sending them on conversational detours to nowhere.

Despite herself, Emma found his quilting plans quite creative. Kevin already had pieced a block featuring a jester's hat for *As You Like It*, a mask for *Much Ado About Nothing*, and a profile of twins for *Comedy of Errors*. They discussed possible additional blocks as they wandered through the rest of the display.

Kelly's stomach brought them back to reality. "It's past one thirty. Don't you think it's time for lunch?"

"I know you think so." Emma sent a commiserating glance toward Kevin before she realized it. He grinned, and she recognized with a shock that sometime that day, he had morphed in her mind from "Crawford" to "Kevin."

He did what they'd expected—reached into a shirt pocket and offered Kelly his bag of soy nuts. "I guess I don't eat out much."

"Kevin, I can't subsist on just a snack." Kelly parked her small frame in front of him, puppy-dogged her eyes, and pleaded, "Before we came inside, I saw an awesome-looking deli down the street. You wouldn't want a New York tourist to go without a stacked-to-the-sky corned-beef-on-rye, would you? You need one too. My treat."

Kelly's everlasting appetite often annoyed Emma, but she could see Kevin weakening at this appeal from a damsel in digestive distress.

"I skipped breakfast this morning," Emma added. Lately,

she had bypassed her bowl of granola, but Kevin didn't have to know that.

"OK. If you guys are hungry, we can go to the deli."

Walking through the heavy glass door of the classic Jewish restaurant with its crowded wooden tables, chairs, and photo-covered walls, Emma was reminded of one of her favorite movies, *When Harry Met Sally.*

To Emma's surprise, several customers asked Kevin for autographs. He complied, but his mouth tightened. Several held up their phones to take pictures.

"No cameras." Kevin clenched his teeth. He looked as if he'd like to grab his fans' phones and smash them.

"Let's find a table." Kelly gently tugged him away.

When they sat, he sighed. "Sometimes I get sick of it all. Exploring Roman was great. Few people, and nobody there recognized me."

Emma hadn't realized autograph hounds would seek him here. Fellow diners still eyed them. Emma buried her nose in the menu. Glancing sideways, she saw Kevin wipe his menu—and his hands—with sanitizer before he opened it.

Afterward, even Kevin admitted lunch was delicious, though he clung to his water bottle. However, he rejected the superiority of Kelly's beloved corned beef. "Pastrami's the best. On crusty French bread, with provolone."

"You don't know what you're missing." But even Kelly struggled to finish her huge sandwich. "Piled to the sky" described it perfectly.

Emma had trouble with her chicken salad too, mostly because she tried to keep a constant DNA vigil without staring.

Once, when her gaze followed Kevin's paper napkin to his lips, his eyes met hers. Emma flushed as if she'd picked his pocket.

Nevertheless, her pulse pounded as she eyed it, crushed in a ball, on his crockery plate.

"Excuse me, ladies," Kevin rose as if he'd read their cue for him to exit. He headed for the men's room.

One, two, three, four. When he'd taken four steps away from the table, both Emma and Kelly reached for his plate.

A way-too-efficient server's hands swept it and their own dishes away.

Noooo. Emma leaped to her feet and lunged after him. Her right foot grabbed a nearby chair leg.

She fell like a tree.

As Kelly helped her up, she saw a diner hold up his phone. Another held up hers.

Heat shot up to her hairline, and Emma knew she was turning red. Fire-engine-cinnamon-red-hot-Dottie-Faye-lipstick red.

"Am I subtle enough?" Emma muttered.

"Kevin's gone. He won't have a clue," Kelly reassured her.

When he returned, Emma dug in her bag, searching for fictional breath mints so he couldn't see her face.

Fortunately, Kevin expected a conference call. "The producer of another comedy, *Twelfth Night*, is interested in me." He shrugged. "I'd rather do *Hamlet*. But it's Shakespeare."

"I'm sure you'll be wonderful in anything." *Let's go home. Please.*

His face lit up, and after they left the deli, he said, "You've seen my show, but would you like to come again? I have two front section tickets for tomorrow night, and we could do something afterward."

A reprieve. Emma said, "I'd love to."

"Great." Kevin handed her the tickets. "I haven't had so much fun in ages. It's not every day I can talk about my Shakespeare quilt without people rolling on the floor, laughing."

Male quilters did experience prejudice when it came to their art. Walter would understand Kevin's quandary. Emma squelched a twinge of sympathy as they waved goodbye.

Watching his retreating back, Kelly nudged Emma. "If he wasn't a suspect in two murders, I'd send you to the show tomorrow night without me. That guy likes you. A lot."

"Oh, please." Emma groaned. "You're letting your romantic side carry you away, Dottie Junior."

She strode toward the subway station. Kelly jogged beside her. Like characters on a kid's video game, they maneuvered down the crowded street.

"Kevin seems nice, but he could be dangerous." There was no kidding in Kelly's face now. "Don't tune him out—you do that with guys. Pay attention to the cues he gives you. And someone needs to be with you two at all times."

"Don't worry." Emma gentled her voice. "I have no intention of ending up a victim—his or anyone else's. Everything he says and does will pass through that filter."

"Good." Kelly gave her a thumbs-up. "Let's go rest our poor, aching feet at Lucinda's."

Emma, too, looked forward to quiet time sewing in the three-season room. Riding the subway, she wished they'd been able to draw Kevin out about Rose. He didn't seem to remember her at all.

Or he was lying for a very good—actually, a very bad—reason.

nine

"I know you'll stick close to Emma—"

A violent "Aah-*chooo!*" exploded Kelly's sentence. She sniffled, "I'm glad you asked Kevin if Dottie Faye could take my place." She sneezed again, burying her nose in her elbow so as not to spray Emma and her aunt, who were dressed up to attend Kevin's show. "Too bad we're not trying to collect my DNA."

Emma wanted to hug her poor, congested friend, swathed in a quilt in Lucinda's guest room. But on the other hand, Emma didn't want to catch Kelly's cold.

"Don't worry. Aunt Dottie will guard me like a dragon," she said, handing her aunt's ticket to her. "You just concentrate on getting well."

"*Dottie Faye* will do fine, Emma Jane," her aunt said, pursing her lipsticked mouth, "and I don't appreciate the comparison. But yes, Kelly Ann, be assured that as I live and breathe, no sneaky, Shakespeare-quoting Yankee will dare touch my niece."

As they left, Emma realized she feared Dottie's possible course of action tonight more than any criminal's. Emma wanted to cultivate Kevin's friendship further, gain his confidence so she could covertly collect his DNA. In Dottie's present mood, she might knock out his teeth and send them to her quickie lab.

Sitting in the taxi, though, her aunt looked elegant, wearing her sleek navy dress, cape, and veiled hat with its long, curved feather. Perhaps Dottie's ladylike attire would inspire her to act the part.

Emma and Dottie entered The Paddington Theater, skirted the remodeling construction around the lobby elevators, and let the untouched red-carpeted lobby do its magic.

Though Emma had seen the show before, a familiar tingle of anticipation zigzagged through her. Everything about musical theater enchanted her—the costumes, the sets, the characters, and especially Kevin's memorable solos. *If only I didn't have to think about murder tonight.*

Someone jammed a microphone under Emma's nose, halting her in her tracks.

"Ms. Cotton, can you tell our *Celebrity Lives* audience what it's like to date Kevin Crawford, off-Broadway's most eligible and elusive bachelor?" A young man wearing a carefully casual suit and calculating smile stood two steps too close.

"We are not dating." Emma sidestepped the meddler and his mic and continued.

Two more arms, wielding microphones, barred her way. "We hear you're from a small town. What do you think of Kevin's world, and how often does he visit yours?"

Emma ducked inside a nearby restroom. Before the door closed behind her, though, Dottie Faye turned on the Southern belle charm: "Please excuse Emma Jane. My niece has always been a teensy bit shy."

Emma groaned and locked herself inside a stall, in case any pursuers were female. *Now what?* They might stake out the restroom indefinitely.

"Just what I need," she muttered. If Kevin knew the media had made them a couple, he might add ten deadbolts to his dressing room door. Not that she'd blame him.

Emma listened. Several pairs of heels wandered through

the restroom, none with the sharp staccato of Dottie's stilettos. Where was she? Still outside the door, sharing the family history with the paparazzi? Emma scowled. Who knew what stories her aunt would dredge up? Hopefully, Dottie wouldn't inform them that Emma would have been prom queen if Tiffany Newsom hadn't gone and broken her leg, thereby winning the sympathy vote.

However, if her aunt really warmed up her vocal cords, she'd scare those professional gossips away in no time. Emma's frown faded, and she couldn't help grinning.

She checked her watch and waited. And waited.

No Dottie.

Kevin had expected them five minutes ago. Slowly Emma emerged from the stall. She saw no one but the gray-haired woman cleaning mirrors, who smiled. "Rotten date? This early in the evening?"

Emma grinned. "No. I'm just a friend of Kevin Crawford's. I'm supposed to see him before his show, but the paparazzi are camped out in the lobby."

"They can't take a hint. Some act downright rude." The janitor finished and stuffed her cloth into a jeans pocket. "Maybe I can help." She pulled an enormous ring of keys from another pocket and opened a closet door. She pointed. "You can leave through the rear door. It opens into a service hallway that leads to the back stairs and the dressing rooms. Even the actors have to use them tonight." The woman clicked her tongue. "Those construction guys move from floor to floor without any rhyme or reason."

Emma hesitated a millisecond. Meet with Kevin alone? But she hurried to the closet. "Thanks! I thought I'd have to spend the night in that stall!"

She followed the janitor past shelves of cleaning supplies

and out the rear door into a bare white corridor. What would Dottie Faye do when she discovered Emma had disappeared? She'd probably notify the FBI, the military, plus her Mary Kay lady. *I'll wish Kevin luck, then call her.*

When they reached his dressing room, the janitor offered, "I'll leave those supply doors unlocked awhile in case you need them."

Emma thanked her rescuer. She reminded herself not to tell Kevin about the media guys, then rapped on the door. He opened it, delight flooding his face.

"Sorry I'm late. Dottie Faye and I were separated, and I need to find her. I just wanted to say 'Break a leg!'"

"Since you're here, I'll put on my best show ever." If possible, his smile broadened. "The overture won't begin for fifteen minutes, and I don't appear until the second act, you know.

"Herbie made coffee again," he continued. "He said he'd join us if he can." Kevin cocked his head in that odd yet captivating way he had. "Dottie Faye knew you would come here before the show, didn't she?"

Yes, she did. Emma paused. Her aunt had not pursued or called *her.* Dottie probably was giving an interview to *The New York Times.* Herbie would soon reappear, achieving a safe three's-company quorum. Emma entered. "Coffee would be nice."

Selecting a clear mug from the table, Emma told herself she couldn't miss another opportunity to understand what made Kevin Crawford tick. Or another chance to harvest his DNA. She'd slip into the theater during the overture to reconnect with Dottie Faye, who probably was posing for photographs by now.

"Kelly really wanted to come," Emma said, mostly to keep their silence from growing awkward. "But she could hardly breathe without sneezing."

At the very mention, Kevin sanitized his hands. But he

suggested chamomile tea with lemon to clear her throat—"I use it all the time." Emma noted the tea as a possibility that might tempt him away from the water bottle he sipped tonight, as usual. They talked pleasantly about Roman Originals. Kevin asked her advice about stitch possibilities for his Shakespeare quilt. Herbie didn't show, but Emma didn't sweat his absence. No conflicting ripples of apprehension disturbed their conversation. Again, Emma asked herself why Herbie had worried about Kevin and whether her suspicions were not only unfounded, but a bit paranoid.

The first strains of the overture swelled overhead.

"I should go." She rose.

"Come afterward and bring Dottie Faye," Kevin urged.

"I'll see how tired she is." *Ha. She can out-party me every time. Click.*

Emma looked over her shoulder, grinning. "What was that noise? Is The Paddington haunted by ghosts?"

For the first time, the smile left his eyes. "Several. The exorcisms haven't been very successful."

While Emma chewed on that odd remark, Kevin crossed the room and turned the doorknob, then rattled it. "The stupid thing's stuck," he said through clenched teeth.

He banged on the door, then pounded on it with a ferocity that startled Emma. "I can't yell for help. It might disrupt the first act."

So might the pounding. And missing your cue. "Maybe you could call a maintenance guy?"

He whirled and snapped, "I didn't bring my phone. I hate phones, and I never make calls right before a performance."

Kevin yanked on the doorknob again. Beads of sweat popped out on his forehead, and he eyeballed her as if the locked door were her fault.

OK. Trying to chuckle, she pulled her phone from her bag. "I'll call Dottie Faye. She'll be only too happy to play superhero and rescue us—especially if someone posts it on Facebook a few hundred times." Emma tried to flick on her phone—dead as a doornail.

Or dead as Rose and Brett?

"Emma strikes again." She tried to keep her tone relaxed. "Kelly is always on me to charge my phone, but she got sick and didn't remind me this time."

Kevin paced as Emma pulled a fingernail file from her evening bag. *Don't get too close, Mister Neurotic.* She knelt by the door. A modern deadbolt had been installed—unlocked, as expected. She began to poke at the old-fashioned mechanism on the doorknob. "I'll bet somebody pennied us in."

"Pennied us in?" He almost snarled. "What does that mean?"

An island of anger erupted in Emma's sea of fear, but she kept her tone light. "Didn't anyone ever penny you into your dorm room?" She edged the file into the lock, jiggling it gently. "Pennies are pushed between the door and the jam above and below the knob until the door won't open. Almost impossible to extract."

"Why would anyone do that?" Kevin paced faster. His moist skin had paled to the light gray of his haunted eyes. "Why would they lock us in?"

"As a joke maybe," Emma said.

"A *joke*?"

She almost mentioned how Kelly had once pennied in an obnoxious admirer, but she swallowed the words before Kevin could insinuate something from them.

The lights blinked out. No window. Only a pencil-thin line of light under the entrance.

Great. Emma let her head fall forward, bumping it on the heavy old door.

She forgot the pain, though, as Kevin let out a primal scream.

ten

Kevin's baritone seemed to desert him. He shrieked, "I gotta get out of here!"

Emma clutched her nail file. *Dottie Faye, where on earth are you?* So much for her aunt's protective mode.

She heard Kevin smash his fists on the door. "Help! *Help!*"

No answer to his subhuman scream. She remembered that Kevin's dressing room, per his request, was located far from the others. *Maybe you don't have to worry about disrupting the show.*

"When you don't appear for your scene, they'll come and find you," she tried to calm him.

"Shut up!"

In the darkness, he sounded like a maniac. Emma shrank into a corner, keeping her file pointed outward. As he battered and bellowed, she slipped her left stiletto from her foot, readying it for combat, if necessary.

After what seemed hours, a thump reverberated at the door. A voice growled, "Kevin? Where in thunder have you been?"

"Somebody locked me in, Jack!" Kevin yelled. "Please, please, get me out of here!"

The stage manager. Emma's memory pinpointed the man's identity. She wilted with relief.

Small clinkings and clankings, muttered maledictions from Jack, and soon a large rectangle of light illuminated the dressing room. Kevin stumbled into the hall, his leafy crown askew.

"Brannigan's probably sent Landon onstage by now, but go, go!" Jack shoved Kevin toward the stage door.

Emma watched him charge down the hall like a wild mustang newly freed. She rose shakily, brushed off her favorite teal and silver dress, and stepped out.

Jack's jaw dropped. Then his eyebrows arched, and he glanced sideways in the universal "Whoa, what was going on here?" expression.

First those jerks with their mics in the lobby, and now this. Emma crossed her arms. "Did this look like a romantic rendezvous?"

Still holding the penny he'd jockeyed from the door, Jack considered, then frowned. "In a word, no."

"Kevin obviously suffers from severe claustrophobia. Whoever pulled this trick knew that." The resentment that simmered at Kevin's intimidation also boiled at the perpetrator's cruelty. "Do you have any idea who that might be?"

Jack's eyes flickered, but he shook his head. "Theater people fight at the drop of a hat. Probably a woman. Wish there was a rule against actors dating each other." He stooped to pick up his tools. "Excuse me. I've got a stage to run." He strode away.

Dating? Had Madison, Kevin's red-haired former flame, pennied them in because she was jealous? That made no sense at all. *If she doesn't want us together, why would she trap us in a room?*

Emma would think about that later. Right now, she needed to find her aunt. She longed to return to Lucinda's and curl up in a quilt á la Kelly. Surely the media nuts no longer lurked in the lobby. Thank heaven they hadn't discovered her and Kevin locked in that dressing room together.

No more cramped, creepy places. Emma sought the main stairway to the lobby.

A minute later, she stared across a yellow "Danger!" tape at the gaping hole where the stairway had been. Sighing, she turned back to take the service stairway—and froze in her tracks.

Dottie didn't know about the service stairway. She couldn't use the elevators because of the remodeling. Unless someone showed her, she couldn't come to Kevin's dressing room. And she couldn't call since Emma's cellphone was dead. Emma gulped. Dottie probably was out of her mind with worry.

Emma slid out of her heels. Grasping them as she dashed down the hall, she climbed the service stairway and ran to the janitor closet.

Yes! Still unlocked. Emma darted between shelves and sprinted through the restroom with breathless apologies after nearly mowing down a line of women primping at mirrors.

She plunged out into the empty, reverberant lobby and looked about wildly.

No Dottie Faye.

Something told Emma that her aunt was not sitting in her seat, placidly enjoying the show. But she had to check anyway. Emma slipped on her shoes and headed for the nearest double doors.

"Ma'am, you may not enter until intermission." A skinny, solemn young man whose tie probably outweighed him planted himself firmly in front of the entrance.

Emma considered mowing him down. Instead, she clasped her hands. "I'm sorry, but I'm looking for my aunt, who's wandered away. She's somewhat elderly ..." *And she could knock you over with her powder puff.*

The usher's eyes widened. "Do you have any idea where she might be?"

Emma handed him her ticket. "We went to the restroom. She may simply have returned to her seat, next to mine, near the front."

The usher bit his lip and then said, "I'll allow you to quietly stand in the back and look. If you'll describe her, I'll check her seat from a vantage point that won't distract the audience."

"She looks younger than she is—tall, blond, wearing a navy dress and hat with a long, curved feather on it. Most of the time, she's quite lucid." Emma wrung her hands. "But occasionally ..."

"I understand." The usher opened the door noiselessly.

No, you don't understand. She slipped into the auditorium, hating her deception. But wasn't she telling the truth to some degree? No one could predict what Dottie Faye might do.

As Emma's eyes grew accustomed to the darkness and the stage lighting, she noted that Landon, Kevin's understudy, was singing Puck's signature song. So Kevin hadn't made it in time.

She couldn't dwell on that. Emma searched the front rows. No glimmer of light reflected from Dottie's blond chignon. No sleek feather silhouette appeared, outlined by a spotlight. Had her aunt gone home?

Emma slipped out, shutting the theater door as noiselessly as the usher did. She turned and almost fell over him.

His lips had pressed into a thin, correct line. "Ma'am, would you come with me? I may have found your aunt."

"Wonderful!" *I think.* As Emma trailed behind the usher, though, a small undertow of uneasiness in her stomach threatened to turn into a tsunami. He did not lead her to the ticket office or a first-aid station. Instead, Emma followed him into a room in the back of the lobby labeled with a brass plate: SECURITY.

"Emma Jane Cotton. Where have you been?" Dottie Faye leaped to her feet and pushed past a uniformed security guard.

Emma threw her arms around her aunt, emotions choking her words. "I'm glad you're all right, Aunt Dottie."

For once, Dottie Faye didn't correct her. "And I thank the good Lord you're in one piece, sweet pea." She framed Emma's face in her hands and kissed her cheeks. "But whatever happened to you? When I checked that restroom, you'd disappeared as if flying saucers had beamed you up."

"Excuse me, ma'am." The guard leveled a flinty look at Emma. "This woman is your aunt?"

"Yes." Emma looked from his stony face to the fireworks that exploded in Dottie's eyes. "Is something wrong, officer?"

"You might say that." The man pronounced each word as if in a courtroom. "She walked onstage during the performance."

"Aunt Dottie!" Emma covered her mouth.

"Don't you 'Aunt Dottie' me, Emma Jane." She crossed her arms. "Such a fuss over nothing. I was just part of the background."

Dottie Faye never faded into the background. "How could you do that?" Emma asked.

"Watch your tone, young lady." Dottie stuck her nose within an inch of Emma's. "I couldn't find you anywhere, and I was worried sick. The show had started, and I figured Kevin was backstage, so I went there to ask him where you'd gone." With an injured air, she sat again. "He wasn't on that side, so I took off my hat, grabbed a long cape thing, and kind of mingled with the Greek people so I could reach the other side."

"She did *not* mingle," the security guard broke in. "I thought she'd never shut up."

SOS. The tsunami rolled over Emma. "You spoke onstage?"

Dottie Faye regarded her perfect nails with satisfaction. "A few itsy-bitsy lines. I offered the king and queen a drink from my water jar."

"I must have missed that part." The usher looked as if he might faint.

Emma wanted to. *I must get Dottie Faye out of here. Now.*

"The audience loved it. They needed a little laugh." Dottie Faye's mouth tightened. "You still have not explained where you were, Emma Jane."

"Somebody pennied Kevin and me into his dressing room."
The minute Emma said it, she knew she shouldn't have.

"'Pennied' you?" The guard now regarded her with the
same "You're insane" look he gave Dottie. "What's that?"

"Ask Kevin." Emma pressed a hand into Dottie's shoulder.
"My aunt really isn't well. I should take her home."

Grasping the cue, Dottie blinked long lashes and said with
childlike innocence, "Do we have enough pennies, Emma
Jane? Enough for bubble gum at Billy Bob's store on the way?"

"Take her home." The guard all but pushed them out
the door.

Emma grasped Dottie's hand. The older woman turned to
smile at the guard. "I'm gonna buy five pieces of bubble gum."

Emma tugged Dottie Faye across the lobby and out the door.

"And my high school drama coach said I couldn't act."
Sunday-dinner–sized satisfaction spread across Dottie's face.
She loosened her hand from Emma's.

Emma mentally juggled words. Finally she answered, "You
outdid yourself, Dottie Faye."

"I certainly did." Her smile faded a little. "Except I left my
hat at the theater."

"Buy another one." Could they ever show their faces at
The Paddington again? Not that Emma wanted to, after Kevin's
meltdown.

"But I loved that hat. It was an original, of course." Dottie
sighed. "Perhaps I can talk Zia into making me another."

Whatever. Suddenly exhausted, Emma could hardly raise
her hand to hail a taxi.

The cabbies seemed to sense her desperation. They zoomed
past like NASCAR contenders.

"Let me do that." Dottie Faye assumed a runway pose and
flashed a smile.

The next taxi stopped. Too tired to feel anything but relief, Emma climbed in. Dottie Faye, in a honeyed tone, directed the driver to Lucinda's address. "Could you step on it, sugar? My niece isn't feeling well tonight."

eleven

"Emma, I'm s-so s-sorry about last night."

She'd never heard Kevin stutter. Emma's fingers tightened around her phone. "I'm sorry it happened too."

Kelly, less snuffly and sewing in their cozy sitting room with Emma, glanced up from her quilt block. Emma gave her an "It's him" nod.

"I know I behaved abominably—"

"You did," Emma snapped.

"I ... just can't stand being locked into a s-space without windows," Kevin pleaded. "It makes me ... a little crazy."

A "little"? What else makes you a "little" crazy? Emma stewed, but she knew she shouldn't drive him away. "We all freak out sometimes. I hate to fly."

"You too?" His voice brightened.

"Thankfully, nobody's locked me in a plane yet." She closed her eyes, trying not to picture it.

He gave a fake chuckle. "I feel terrible about my behavior, though. Is there s-some way I can make it up to you?" He paused. "Probably not free tickets, right?"

"Right." Surely he'd heard about Dottie Faye's fiasco.

He chuckled again, sounding more like himself. "Your aunt made quite an impression."

"She usually does."

To Emma's relief, Kevin changed the subject. "The Metropolitan Museum of Art is featuring an Asian quilt exhibition. I haven't checked out their costume gallery lately. Would you, Kelly, and Dottie Faye like to go Tuesday? My treat."

"I'll check with them." Emma covered her phone and told Kelly about Kevin's invitation.

"That's what we're here for, right?" Kelly whispered. "Sorry to crash your 'date,' but after last night, I'll be glad to go."

Emma returned the phone to her ear. "The museum sounds good." *Though going with you doesn't.* They worked out a time and place.

After Emma hung up, Kelly paused in her project. "So ... you survived Dottie Faye, and you've had a chance to sleep on this whole thing ...."

"Sort of." Emma's brain had ground its gears for hours. She hadn't dozed off until three o'clock and needed a double espresso to jump-start her at eight. "Perhaps we should have told Kevin from the beginning why we're in New York."

"That didn't work with Allyson or Shay." Kelly reminded her about the two former students from Rose's class they'd already investigated. "It nearly wrecked everything."

"You're right." Emma flopped into her chair.

"Maybe you don't feel like talking about Kevin and Rose right now." Kelly returned to embroidering a block of a photo quilt she hoped to finish by spring.

"No, when my mind's spinning, talking with you helps clarify things." Emma fingered a poinsettia she was piecing for a Christmas wall hanging. "Ask me questions, Kelly."

"OK. The obvious: Who would lock you and Kevin in his dressing room?"

"I'm not sure the person knew I was there—or cared." Emma began to stitch her pieces.

"You're assuming the prankster wanted to lock Kevin in?"

"Yes." Emma gave her a curious look. "Why would anyone do that to me?"

"It doesn't make sense," Kelly admitted. "Our identity thief stuck it to you—and me—the logical way. If he wanted to scare you off this case, he'd find some other way to do it. Pennying you in with Kevin? I don't think so."

"Although that wasn't fun and games." Emma shook her head. "Kevin acted like a trapped animal." She shuddered.

"Did he threaten you?"

"Not in so many words." Emma trimmed threads from a fraying edge. "But I didn't know what he'd do next." She squelched her fears. "As long as we stay together and avoid quiet corners at the museum, I think we'll be safe. But we'll have to keep our guard up."

"This penny-in incident may have nothing whatsoever to do with you, with us, or with Rose's death." Kelly mused. "When you and Kevin got out, Kevin realized his costume and props had been taken. Do you think the person who locked you in might somehow be connected with Brett Damon's death? That seems like a long shot, but it might be something to consider."

"I think Madison Leigh is behind it," Emma said. "She's Kevin's ex-girlfriend, remember? Herbie said she accused Kevin of keeping her from getting roles she wants. Plus, she probably knows him well enough to exploit his claustrophobia." Again, anger smoldered in Emma at the malice that must have planned Kevin's meltdown.

"That works." Kelly pulled another block from her project bag. "Of course, she had nothing to do with Rose's death, regardless of her past relationship with Kevin. Madison's probably twenty-five?"

Emma nodded. "Far too young to have been the female involved. But the woman who was involved in Rose's death may be afraid Kevin will implicate her. Perhaps she mistakenly had Brett killed."

"Why would she have waited all these years?" Kelly wondered.

"Maybe she just now found him, though Kevin wouldn't have been hard to track recently. Or maybe he's kept their vow of silence—until now."

"This is growing more complicated by the minute." Kelly shook her head.

One thing at a time. Emma steered their discussion back to the dressing room prank. "The timing of the lock-in bothers me. Whatever her motive, could Madison have pennied us in and cut the lights, then showed up onstage in time for Act II, when she had to do her fairy thing?"

"Did the lock-in and lights-out happen simultaneously?" Kelly probed.

"No, I remember a short interval between them." Emma tried to recall how long. "If the electric box were close to Kevin's dressing room, she could pull it off."

"Although some computer programs enable people to control lights," Kelly said. "Maybe she's an expert hacker. Or knows one."

Emma grimaced. "Technology always confuses things."

"Only if you make it your enemy." Kelly wagged a finger.

"We're wandering off topic. So … let's get acquainted with Madison. I'll bet she has a fan page on Facebook. I'll call Cat Simon; she's always in the know about the latest gossip in the theater world. And we can talk to Herbie."

"Though he might not give us the most objective report." Kelly grinned. "He seems smitten with Madison."

"I think we should take turns following her the next few days. We might learn a bit about what makes her tick."

"I could get Reed to talk about her." Dottie Faye's

voice forced three inches of air between Emma and the chair. Her aunt stepped through the door. "I'm good at that, you know."

How could they have forgotten Dottie's mom-like omnipresence? How much had she overheard? Emma blended her aunt's intrusion in as smoothly as she could. "Yes, you are. Good idea. As ga-ga as Herbie is about Madison, he's probably tried to get his dad to represent her. At any rate, I'm sure Reed's familiar with her."

Emma gestured at the chair beside her, and Dottie sat, sweet smile dripping smugness.

"But I don't think you should follow her, Dottie Faye," Emma cautioned. "Madison probably remembers you from your off-Broadway debut the other night."

"I was unforgettable, wasn't I?" Dottie Faye's smile stretched to impossible proportions. She patted her hair.

Kelly interjected, "Madison might remember you too, Emma, if she's still hot on Kevin."

"I doubt it, but maybe I'd better take night shifts."

"Sneaking around New York at night by yourself?" Dottie demanded, righteous anger rising with her perfectly plucked eyebrows. "I don't think so, sweet pea."

Emma hated to admit it, but her aunt had a point. "Um ..."

"I know!" Dottie's "Eureka!" smile, the one they feared most, appeared. "I'll wear my hot dog–stand wig and go with you." She swept a hand to include Kelly. "We can all use Dottie Cams! Color coordinated with our outfits, of course. Y'all will look so cute with them in your hair."

Emma's mouth wobbled, but no words formed. Wear a neon-colored plastic-flower video camera her aunt had purchased over the Internet? Amazingly, they had played a somewhat helpful role when Dottie pushed her way into earlier investigations of Rose's case. Though the floral spyware probably glowed in the dark, they wouldn't record well at night—

"I might take you up on that, Dottie Faye, if you'll show me how they work," Kelly said.

Had her partner lost her mind? Worse yet, had Kelly adopted Dottie's fashion sense?

"Videos would keep me from missing important details," Kelly continued placidly, despite Emma's lightning-bolt glance. "I could use one during the day, but they might not work at night."

"I used them one evening," Dottie retorted, "and though the video's a little fuzzy and a teensy bit bouncy, it caught a lot. Besides, the lights are always on in New York." She studied Emma. "You'll need a wig too. Blondes catch the eye, you know."

"I'll wear a hat."

"I know exactly the perfect wig for you. I'll order it right now. Overnight shipping." Dottie Faye gleefully headed for her room and computer.

Great. "No big hair, do you understand?" Emma called after her, and then put away her sewing. "I need air."

A brisk jog through Lucinda's manicured neighborhood helped Emma breathe again. But for a week of all-night stakeouts, trapped in her Jeep with Dottie Faye, would she require an oxygen tank?

"I didn't think a stakeout meant watching stoplights change." Dottie, a dark blue flower bobby-pinned to her wig, yawned and stretched her long legs in the passenger seat of Emma's Jeep. "And I'm freezing to death."

Emma started the heater again. She sipped coffee, trying to forget the flower pinned to her mousy brown 1980s locks.

"Doing nothing is making me crazy," Dottie continued grousing. "The most exciting thing my Dottie Cam has caught tonight is Madison's roommate coming home and a sleeping cat."

Emma thought of other sections of New York where she wouldn't dare drive, let alone park. She touched a can of Mace in her pocket. "Maybe we should be glad?"

Madison's neighborhood seemed quiet by New York standards. Everlasting traffic grumbled in the background, of course, with occasional screams from fire trucks and police cars. But at only ten thirty, few people came and went from this aged limestone apartment building, a look-alike of those in surrounding blocks. Not what Emma had expected in "The City That Never Sleeps."

Late after Sunday night's show, she and her aunt, Dottie Cams running, had followed Madison to a convenience store. They recorded her eating a slice of pizza and buying hair spray. Today Kelly had reported that Madison had shopped and done errands all afternoon. She returned home around four thirty. As there was no performance on Monday nights, she'd stayed home. Not surprising, given her antisocial personality. Kelly had imposed on Herbie to gain admittance into rehearsals. She'd noticed Madison rarely talked to anyone during breaks, occasionally snarling at Landon Green. How had she and Kevin, two loners, ever found each other?

Emma glanced in her rearview mirror and side mirrors. She felt for the Mace again and fingered the small tool kit in her other coat pocket that she'd brought along for unknown emergencies. Anything could happen. But "nothing" seemed more likely.

"Did you know that if I eat two hundred blackened watermelon seeds every day, I'll never have a weight problem?" Dottie Faye, tired of videoing the cat, had resorted to Googling "fat burners" on her pink phone.

"No, I didn't." So let her aunt amuse herself. Given the current level of excitement, Emma could watch the building.

She stiffened, though, as the front door opened. Streetlight beams reached for Madison's red-gold hair.

"Probably another pizza run." Dottie Faye didn't raise her eyes from her phone. "This girl's social life would bore Mother Teresa."

This time, however, Madison walked half a block to a busier corner and hailed a taxi. Emma barely started her Jeep before the taxi pulled into traffic.

"Follow her, Emma Jane." Dottie leaned forward, her nose almost to the windshield.

"I am, I am." Emma zoomed, swerved, even screeched as she tried to keep Madison's taxi in sight. So much for staying incognito. She marveled that several police cars ignored her wild antics. *But then,* she reminded herself, *everyone in New York drives like this.*

If only they were chasing this woman in Mystic Harbor. Emma knew every dip of every road there. Probably every car in town too.

Emma never had cornered on two wheels before, but she surprised herself by making a clean landing. Panting as the Jeep roared on, she cast a glance sideways to see if she'd frightened her aunt.

"Wooooo-hoo!" Dottie Faye whooped, her wig flopping up and down. "Go get her, Emma Jane!"

Emma slid around a last corner, only to discover Madison's taxi had stopped.

In front of a church.

A large, venerable church surrounded by an old cemetery, with a school across the street. Emma pulled over, amazed to find an expensive but legal parking space nearby. Meanwhile, Madison jumped from the taxi, paid the driver, and hurried away.

"She's going to *church?*" Dottie Faye sounded almost disappointed.

"At eleven o'clock? I don't think so." Emma flicked her overhead light switch to "off" before opening the Jeep's door. "Maybe

Madison's having an emergency meeting with the pastor."

"She's walking right past the church door." Dottie climbed out of the Jeep faster than any woman her age had a right to.

Emma noted that Madison also ignored a lighted sign indicating the church name and office. *Bronson Street Lutheran.* Together she and Dottie Faye crossed the street to the dense though leafless hedge that ran to the end of the block.

Emma, squinting between bushes, saw the shadowy safety-light silhouette of a woman walking steadily on a path among surreally lit gravestones. Dottie Faye on her heels, Emma hurried to the end of the hedge. She halted. Her aunt didn't.

Dottie's pointy-toed shoes jammed into Emma's Achilles tendons. Emma injured her lower lip herself, biting it to keep from crying out.

In the darkness, her aunt pantomimed an apology. Emma pointed to a path under ancient, bony trees, hoping its loop went Madison's direction. They walked in silence, the autumn night's chilly mists wafting the damp smell of aged limestone in their faces.

Madison occasionally disappeared behind bushes and monuments, but inevitably her hair reflected the gleam of streetlights, safety lights, or moonlight.

Emma and Dottie Faye, crouched behind large evergreens, watched Madison head toward the church again. Between its nave and crossing, Emma spotted a bench on which sat a figure, shadows and light playing on his dark, curly hair. Emma couldn't see his face, but something about him seemed familiar. Had she seen his profile before? He rose as Madison quickened her pace, almost running into his arms. They entwined like morning glories for one of the longest kisses Emma had ever witnessed on stage or screen.

Why here, of all places, at night? Emma's cheeks heated. *I feel like a voyeur, sneaking around someone's window.* She longed to slip away, but the chance of escape seemed small.

Eventually the couple, still entwined, wandered toward the alley behind the church. As they turned the corner of the old building, Emma crept from one bush to another, Dottie following. They edged along the church wall, Emma moving faster and faster. Madison and her guy had seemed in no hurry, so surely they'd find them before they took a taxi or drove away.

Emma peeked around the corner and spotted them crossing the street. A streetlight shone on the duo like a spotlight, and Emma gasped.

"What is it?" Dottie's voice pushed Emma almost palpably.

A passing city bus blocked Emma's view. She dashed forward and ducked behind an evil-smelling dumpster, hoping for a better vantage point. But after the bus lumbered by, the couple had vanished.

Emma hurried up the alley, occasionally flattening herself against the cold church wall. Dottie followed her movements like a shadow. But the street seemed almost as deserted as the cemetery. She exhaled a breath of frustration—and of triumph.

Dottie Faye, puffing as she caught up, clicked her tongue. "Lost them! I suppose we'd better go back to Madison's apartment and watch stoplights change again."

"You're probably right."

Dottie's potent blue glance probed her. "Emma Jane, why are you smiling like the coon that ate the corn?"

Emma let her grin widen. "Because I recognized Madison's boyfriend. Not somebody we'd expect."

"Don't keep me in suspense. My feet hurt, and my makeup needs fixing."

At midnight? "Remember that Kelly said Madison hardly talked to anyone except one guy? And she griped at him."

Dottie Faye sputtered, "Spit it out, Emma Jane."

"Kevin's new understudy. Landon Green."

twelve

"**K**evin Crawford and I are not dating," Emma told the reporter again. He'd cornered her in the art museum's gift store.

"Of course you aren't." He clicked a photo anyway. And a few more.

"Young man, did you hear her?" Dottie Faye planted herself in front of Emma and glared at him like a gargoyle. "Emma Jane is simply Kevin's friend. You aim that camera at her one more time," she pointed, "and I'll throw it into that fountain for you."

"So you throw cameras like Crawford? Are you his mother?" The man backed away, taking a picture of Dottie. When she raised her sizable purse, he left.

Emma choked down anger and laughter as Kelly emerged from a restroom to find Dottie, with purse upraised, still glowering. "Wow, what happened?"

"Nothing I couldn't handle." Dottie Faye strode toward the information center, where they were to meet Kevin after the break. Emma filled Kelly in as they followed.

Dottie Faye not only had rescued Emma from the reporter, but she also dispatched several autograph seekers dogging Kevin.

"Can I hire you as my bodyguard?" he asked, flashing his chandelier smile.

"I'd be glad to assist you, sir, in any way I can." Dottie fluttered her eyelashes and almost curtsied.

You're starstruck, Dottie Faye. Emma chuckled inwardly. She had no doubt that her aunt, though intent on finding Rose's murderer, still cherished the idea that an association with Kevin might eventually put her own name in lights. Several times, Dottie had mentioned her interest in supporting Kevin's future productions. She even asked him endless questions about the Asian quilt exhibit, though Dottie found quilts uninteresting and mostly attended Nimble Thimble meetings to annoy Maeve. Kevin seemed to like answering, though, and while her aunt kept him occupied, Emma and Kelly enjoyed the magnificent museum and the complex fans, kites, kimonos, and bird motifs of the glorious quilts. Emma jotted down some ideas for new patterns in her sample book—and focused on opportunities to collect Kevin's DNA.

She loaned him tissues when he realized he'd forgotten his handkerchief. But he hunted for a trash can immediately after he used each one, and cleansed his hands with sanitizer. Kevin even took the stairs to another floor when he couldn't find a receptacle on theirs.

He insisted on taking them to afternoon tea at the museum's Petrie Court Café, with its sweeping view of Central Park. There they dined on Croque-Monsieur, petits fours, and Dragon Pearl jasmine tea. But he ate nothing and drank only from his water bottle—to the consternation of their waiter, whom Kevin silenced by volunteering his autograph.

On their way to the subway, Dottie Faye made a final valiant attempt to collect his DNA. "Kevin, I do believe I see a gray hair." She reached toward his temple.

He laughed and ducked her fingers. "You probably see a lot of them. Reed wants me to do something about it, but I don't like dumping chemicals on my head."

That night, Emma and Dottie recapped the day while Dottie brushed her hair.

Emma plucked her right eyebrow. "Too bad we can't do this to Kevin."

Her aunt harrumphed. "I'll find a way to get that DNA. You'll see."

Emma winced, more at the thought than her quick twinge of pain. She didn't want to think about her aunt's next plan. Yet they had to do this. Soon. Emma didn't want to stay in New York forever.

Her thoughts wandered longingly to Mystic Harbor, where she and Dottie Faye would share Thanksgiving with Kelly's family in a few days.

Her aunt waved a hand before her eyes. "Where are you, sweet pea? You're not thinking about Kevin, are you?" Dottie crossed her arms. "Now you listen to me, Emma Jane. He seems nice—though he may be a killer. But even if he isn't one, he's not a proper Southern gentleman, the kind you deserve. He's good-looking, and he sings like an angel. But he's not for you." She patted Emma's shoulder. "Now Dr. Eric, he's the one you should be dreaming about."

Emma listened. And plucked occasional hairs. And nodded.

She wasn't dreaming about Kevin. Or Eric. Or any gentleman, proper, Southern, or otherwise.

She was dreaming about the day she could solve these murders and go home for good.

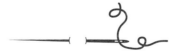

For one blessed, relaxing day, Emma feasted with her Mystic Harbor friends and forgot about collecting DNA. Spending a quiet night in her own bed rested her even more than she'd anticipated.

But the next day, she visited the police station.

"We haven't made much progress in tracking down your

identity thief." Boyer's mouth tightened when Emma entered his cluttered cubicle. Now his lips flattened until they all but disappeared. "Whoever did this sure knew how to hide his tracks. The leads we've checked have gone nowhere. Even our experts are puzzled."

"Kelly and I have changed our credit cards, banking numbers, and passwords. We keep a close eye on our accounts." Emma tried to keep her voice pleasant. Antagonizing the man again would only complicate matters. "Should we do anything else?"

"Watch each other's back." Boyer's concerned expression surprised her into silence. "We check on your shop and your property on a regular basis. We don't want any more fires."

Their first witness in Rose's murder case, Allyson Vernon, had taken desperate measures to throw Emma and Kelly off what Allyson thought was their attempt to ruin her legal career. Emma tried to push the acrid smell of smoke from her memory. "Neither do we."

Boyer leaned forward on his paper-strewn desk. "But we can't protect you in New York. No one can, really."

A double helix of fear and irritation spiraled through her. "Kelly and I haven't experienced problems with our personal safety. We must stay there until we find out what we need to know."

"And what you 'need' to know involves a case closed fifteen years ago." Sparks of anger exploded the worried look.

"Closed for the sake of convenience," Emma retorted. "Not because anybody solved it."

"This is not some TV detective show, Emma!" Boyer raised his voice, and he thumped his desk for emphasis. A pencil flipped into the air, and Emma almost giggled at the frustration on his face.

But the use of her first name angered her. She hammered

out the words, "I can tell the difference between TV and reality, Boyer."

"I don't think so." He stood, his fiery gaze matching hers. "We are dealing with real criminals who don't care who they hurt. Identity thieves don't usually come after their victims, but I hear around town that you've gotten involved in the death of some New York actor too."

She stood and glared at him. "Kelly and I believe that death may be connected to Rose's case."

"You two are regular lightning rods for trouble."

"Really?" She couldn't control her fury. "At least we don't quit because someone pressures us. We follow through. We do what's right."

He raised his hands, and then let them drop. "I'm doing the best I can, Emma. But if you refuse to budge on this issue, I can't help you."

"As if you ever did." Emma turned her back on Boyer and strode out of the station.

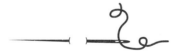

"Why can't you stay all weekend?" Maeve made a sad face as the Nimble Thimbles finished their Saturday session. "It's a holiday, after all. You'll miss the Christmas Gala tonight."

"Dr. Eric would take her, but Emma Jane *has* to return to New York." Dottie Faye didn't hide her disgust.

"I need to check on a lead we've been pursuing." Emma planned to track Madison again on Sunday. She also wanted to avoid last-minute dates other well-meaning friends might try to set up for her.

Kelly understood. "Follow-up is important—"

"Other things are important too." Dottie sniffed. "Like dancing with the handsomest, nicest Southern gentleman in New England."

"I hate to say it, but Dottie's right, Emma. This is the biggest party of the year." Maeve shook her head. "Sometimes I don't understand you."

Emma folded fabric as if her life depended on it. The other Thimbles covered the conflict with a soothing cloak of conversation while they cleaned up.

"I love my store and Mystic Harbor," Marcia said, "but I wouldn't mind changing places with you girls for a night or two, hobnobbing with Broadway stars."

"It's not as glamorous as it sounds." Emma retrieved scraps from the floor, trying to forget the wig she wore during stakeouts.

The Nimble Thimbles stored their supplies, pleased with their progress on the Pirate Museum quilt. Emma thanked them again for their support, especially in keeping the doors at Cotton & Grace open. She made one last stop by the shop to check on incoming shipments with their Saturday help.

As Emma's Jeep zipped toward New York on Interstate 95 again, she pondered their investigation of Madison and Landon. She'd confirmed neither was a member of the Bronson Street Lutheran Church.

"Surprise, surprise," Emma said aloud, grinning, though she fought traffic. Before Thanksgiving, Emma and Dottie Faye had seen them there again. Kelly also had followed Madison and Landon to a Starbucks in Queens. But no one had seen or heard anything that linked the couple to locking Kevin and her in his dressing room.

Emma's thoughts wandered to Herbie's phone call earlier that very morning. More minor stuff was happening at The

Paddington. "It's made Kevin a little crazy," Herbie reported, "and he's pulled back into his shell."

Emma forgot about Kevin as she maneuvered lanes, exits, and lung-clogging traffic jams. She hadn't counted on darkness closing in before she pulled into the parking garage where Lucinda rented fifth-floor guest spaces. According to Dottie Faye, a constant stream of visitors enjoyed Lucinda's hospitality. *Bless her. I've never seen such a woman!*

She lived only four blocks away. Emma pictured sitting in the three-season room with her hostess, enjoying hot cider and nut bread. Perhaps they'd even see a few stars twinkle through the smog.

Emma pulled her overnight bag from the backseat and slammed the Jeep's door. She ignored the elevator. A jaunt down the stairs would de-paralyze her rear. Emma strode toward the nearest corner stairwell.

Phantom footsteps trailed after her.

Echoes of her own, most likely. This huge, chilly space reminded her more of a cave than a building. Emma swung her bag back and forth, never breaking stride. She yanked the door open, letting it slam behind her. *Take that, Mr. Ghost.*

As she descended, Emma slapped her tennies against the concrete steps, trying to laugh at her eight-year-old brand of bravado.

But another slam and a series of heavy, thudding foot-steps above sent her adrenaline into overdrive. She didn't dare look up.

Don't be paranoid. So somebody else wants exercise too. She forced herself to slow down. She'd let this health-conscious Bigfoot pass her and smile a friendly "Go for it!" as he beat her to the landing.

But the footsteps slowed too.

I didn't imagine them. And I'm not waiting for them. Emma's silent prayer turned into an inner cadence that drove her down the stairs. Though she tried to keep her panicked feet under control, they soon ran wildly as her pursuer drew nearer.

As she dashed down the last flight, she realized he had stopped. She didn't. Neither did the two bricks that flew in front of her and smashed against the wall.

Emma sprinted then, pain exploding in her sides, panting like an animal running for its life.

thirteen

Kevin took Emma's hand as he met her, Kelly, and Herbie outside The Paddington's back exit. "Emma, I'm so glad you're all right. It's a wonder anyone goes out at night in this town, with all the crazies lurking in every alley and parking garage."

A passing actor and two stagehands, well acquainted with Kevin's dislike of touching, smirked as they left. Emma forced a smile and loosened his grip. *What, no sanitizer?* "I'm fine. I reported it to the police, and now I want to forget it."

If only Dottie Faye had kept quiet about her ordeal. But no—she'd probably called all the local TV stations. Kelly had been shaken, returning to the Big Apple to join her friend and partner. She made Emma promise not to navigate New York alone at night.

Kevin frowned. "I heard you were alone when that guy chased you."

"That won't happen again," Kelly spoke up. Emma grimaced. Dottie Faye had threatened to call her father.

"Kevin," Herbie interrupted, "are you sure you won't go with us to Central Park?" He scowled. "Dad shouldn't mess with your plans at the last minute. It's not fair."

"It's part of the business. I can't pass up two major photo ops and an interview." Kevin shrugged, but he sounded as if he were being jailed. "Man, what I wouldn't give to go with you guys." To Emma's annoyance, he reached for her hand again. "Maybe we could go to Central Park too? Early Thursday afternoon?"

Emma dodged his fingers and re-pasted the smile on her face. "That might work."

Fortunately, Dottie Faye announced her arrival with a Southern-belle giggle. "Oh, Reed, you're just the funniest man I know."

The agent grinned at her like a smitten high school sweetheart, but his smile faded at the sight of Kevin. "You do remember you have a one o'clock with *ArtBeat*, don't you?"

"I remember, Reed." Kevin enunciated each word. "You don't have to check on me."

His agent raised his hands in an exaggerated "back off" gesture. "I just brought Dottie Faye here to rendezvous with her group."

"Are you sure you can't join us, Reed?" Dottie cooed.

"I'd love to, but I have a meeting too." He bestowed a light kiss on her cheek and left. Emma exchanged glances with Kelly. Maybe Dottie was too good an actress.

Maybe she wasn't acting?

They ate lunch at a deli. The sun shone—unusual for late November. Emma loved brisk jaunts, but by the time they entered the Conservatory Garden through the ornate Vanderbilt wrought-iron gate, she wanted to sit on a bench, absorb the remaining autumn colors, and enjoy the Italian section's graceful fountain and quiet pool.

Emma didn't feel like talking. Fortunately, Dottie Faye and Herbie competed for chatterbox honors, with Kelly keeping the conversation sane. They gave thumbs-up and -down to off-Broadway's current repertoire.

Emma's thoughts ping-ponged in her head. Kevin had clung to her hand—unusual for him, but then, he *was* an actor. Emma reminded herself that Kevin knew what day she'd planned to return to New York. Could he have been the brick thrower?

He could have tried to intimidate her so she wouldn't ferret out the truth about him. But no, he'd performed that evening. Perhaps Kevin and the mugger were secret best buds. She tried to wrap her mind around that.

Emma heard her name. She swam to the surface of her subconscious. Had someone asked her a question?

"Sweet pea, you've been in a trance all day." Dottie aimed a tickle at her ribs. "Do you need a dose of Granny Murleen's tonic?"

That threat had ensured Emma's health and well-being since her childhood. "I'm good, Dottie Faye." She stood. "I haven't seen the French section of the garden yet. Why don't we go there next?"

Emma set a vigorous pace that defied her aunt's cures. Dottie, following with Kelly, had to put her energy into her stride rather than her mouth. They passed through an arbor, encountering the whimsical Three Dancing Maidens bronze sculpture. Though colder weather had taken its toll on surrounding masses of russet, lavender, yellow, and white Korean chrysanthemums, the flowers still presented a spectacular scene, giving off a faint, woodsy fragrance.

Herbie kept up easily, and he could talk under any circumstances. "I wish you guys could move to New York. I miss you and Kelly when you leave."

Despite his theater sophistication, Herbie sounded like a ten-year-old.

No wonder, with no mom to balance his pushy dad. The events of the last few weeks must have blown Herbie away. "I'm glad we're friends." Emma bopped his arm playfully, as she did with Kelly's college-age son, Keith.

"After what happened to Brett, Dad's been impossible," Herbie said moodily. "I stay out of his way. He's been doing weird things." The boy's few freckles disappeared as he wrinkled his nose. "I saw him last week in a coffeehouse with Landon."

"Landon Green?" At the name, Emma's steps slowed. "Well, your dad *is* an agent."

"Yeah, but he'd never pursue Landon." Herbie snorted. "Dad goes after the winners. Landon's OK, but so are a gazillion other actors."

"He didn't see you?"

"Nah. And I'm sure not going to ask him about it."

Interesting. But significant? Emma wished she could provide answers to all the questions she asked herself. She and Kelly would hash this one out back at Lucinda's.

Herbie, however, wasn't finished baring his soul. "I'm worried about Kevin. Brett's death messed him up, but since somebody locked you guys in his dressing room, he's been more paranoid than ever. He calls me in the middle of the night. He's hardly sleeping at all."

Though she harbored definite reservations about who should worry about whom, the boy's concern touched Emma. "You're a good friend, Herbie, but Kevin needs more help than you can give. If he won't see a counselor, you can't do much about it."

"He'll get better, now that you're back."

Emma's sympathy levels dropped. "He needs more than I can give too. Let's encourage him to get some help."

Her phone trilled, and she stuck it to her ear, glad for an interruption. "Hello?"

"You're not alone, are you, Emma?" No greeting. Just Kevin's anxious baritone.

Like that's your business? She drained irritation from her tone as best she could. "No, I'm still hanging with the gang in the French gardens." *In broad daylight, no less.*

"Nobody's following you?"

She attempted a small chuckle. "If he is, he's out of breath. We're moving at a good pace."

She heard him exhale. "I just wanted to make sure you were OK."

"I'm fine." As she hung up, Emma read the "See what I mean?" in Herbie's dark eyes.

She saw. And she didn't like it.

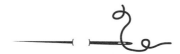

"Emma. Can you come? Now?"

Luxuriating in the Jacuzzi in Lucinda's guest bathroom, Emma wanted to block Kevin's endless calls forever. The extreme panic in his voice made her summon what little patience she still possessed. "What's wrong?"

"Jermaine's really sick. I called 911."

"Who's Jermaine?"

"Jermaine Dole. The understudy for the character Nick Bottom." He sounded almost tearful. "It's all my fault too."

"What?" Now Emma wanted to drown her phone so Kevin's terrified words would die in incoherent bubbles. *Ridiculous. How could you have made Jermaine sick?*

"Meet me at Metro Memorial's ER? Please? Please!"

"Calm down, Kevin. All right—"

"Oh, thank you. See you there."

Click.

Wonderful. Emma flopped back into the tub.

Kelly called, "Are you all right in there?"

No. "I'm OK." Emma crawled out of the Jacuzzi. She threw on a deliciously soft spa robe, the one she'd wanted to wear while giving herself a long, pampering pedicure. "Kevin called. Again."

"I was afraid of that."

Emma trudged into their room and began to dress. "This time, I think he's totally lost it." She told Kelly about Kevin's rantings. "I've hit my limit, Kelly. I can't take this anymore."

By the time they had plowed through rush hour traffic and walked toward the hospital entrance, Kelly had talked her down from the ledge. "If Kevin gets out of control, let me handle him."

"Gladly. Thanks."

"My pleasure." Kelly grinned. "The next time my kids give me fits, I'll sic them on you."

"I get the best part of this deal."

Kelly gestured toward the ER's automatic doors like a maître d'. "You are so right, friend."

They had no time to say more because Kevin, in the middle of a loud argument with the admissions clerk, spotted them. Emma suddenly found herself almost airborne, clasped in Kevin's wiry arms so tightly that she could hardly inhale. "You're here," he murmured.

In an instant, she understood that however demented he'd sounded, Kevin's angst was not imaginary. Gently, she extricated herself. "Can you tell us more about this?"

He made a futile, hostile gesture toward the stony-faced clerk. "I could if they'd let me stay with Jermaine and talk to the doctors. He's all alone back there! But I'm not family—"

"They're trying to take good care of your friend." Kelly patted his shoulder. "We have to keep out of their way so they can do it."

His shoulders sagged. "I suppose you're right."

Kelly gently steered Kevin toward the waiting area. "Let's sit, and you can tell us about Jermaine."

He surprised Emma by taking her up on her offer to find

iced tea for them. Sure enough, she noticed his water bottle's conspicuous absence. He *was* upset.

While feeding the vending machine, she pondered Kelly's ability to quiet him. Though Emma had kept her cool with Kevin—so far—hysterical types made her crazy.

Maybe it's the mother thing.

The moment she handed Kevin his bottle of green tea, a reminder, like her Jeep's lights-off alarm, dinged in her mind.

DNA alert.

Part of Emma shook a finger at herself for thinking of such a thing when Kevin was so vulnerable. But the part that would do anything for Rose won out.

Kevin slumped next to a corner table when Emma returned. She sat on the other side of it. Emma kept her ears open for Kevin's story, and she kept her eyes, with the exception of a few sympathetic looks, on his tea bottle.

He drank a third of it in one gulp. "It started so harmlessly. Jermaine came by my dressing room, asking for feedback on his line delivery. We worked awhile, and he nailed them."

Kevin chugged another drink. Emma watched his long fingers grasp the bottle. "Then some fan sent me this platter of Thai food. I like Thai, but, well, you know I usually don't eat away from home. Jermaine isn't making much money, so I asked if he wanted it. He scarfed it down and practically licked the plate." A muscle worked in his jaw. "With everything that's been going on, I should never have passed it off on him. What was I thinking?" He slammed the bottle on the table and gripped his head in his hands.

OK, DNA or no DNA, Emma found it difficult to picture this sad, miserable man as a murderer or the guy who paid someone to throw bricks at her. Still, she kept the tea bottle in her peripheral vision as she and Kelly patted his arms.

"You were being generous, Kevin." Emma kept her voice warm but level. "I'm sure Jermaine knows that."

"He's a good kid," Kevin muttered. "He works hard. He doesn't deserve this."

Rose didn't deserve what she got, either. Emma lectured herself, How do you know Kevin was being generous? Maybe Jermaine saw or heard something Kevin thought he shouldn't.

Good grief. I'm beginning to think the guy wants to knock off the entire cast. I'm as paranoid as he is.

Or—perhaps Kevin's paranoia wasn't so paranoid. If he was telling the truth about Jermaine, then somebody seriously had it in for Kevin ... depending on how serious Jermaine's illness was. Madison? Or the woman involved in Rose's murder?

Kelly caught her glance and shook her head slightly. Emma knew what her friend meant: "Hold off until we can discuss this."

Fine. Emma's own stomach felt as if it were being pumped. Forcing her eyes back to the tea bottle, she wanted to throw it. At whom? She wasn't sure.

A tired-looking young physician dressed in green scrubs first talked to the admissions clerk, who rolled his eyes, then approached them. "I'm Dr. Rebecca Lindstrom. You're Kevin Crawford, Jermaine Dole's friend?"

Kevin leaped to his feet. "Yes. How is he? Where is he?"

"We've admitted him." Her direct blue eyes, underscored by dark circles, assessed Kevin. "Jermaine gave us permission to share his medical information with you, as he has no family in this area."

"Is he going to be OK?" Kevin's eyes bulged with anxiety, and he wrung his hands. The doctor took a step back. From the look on her face, Emma surmised she did not recognize Kevin. If she did, she certainly wasn't a groupie.

"I expect he'll be fine in a day or two."

Kevin dropped into the vinyl chair like a stringless puppet. "Thank God," he whispered.

Dr. Lindstrom continued, "Jermaine's abdominal pain and other digestive symptoms suggest that the food he ate violently disagreed with him. It could be simple food poisoning, or he might have some food allergy. He's quite dehydrated, so we'll keep him overnight for observation. If he's recovered sufficiently, we'll dismiss him tomorrow."

Kevin moved toward the physician and lowered his face within inches of hers. "Can you tell if someone poisoned the food?"

The doctor's blond eyebrows formed an almost invisible line over her eyes. "Is there reason to suspect that?"

Shall I list all the possibilities? Emma shook her head. "No proof. Just suspicions."

"I think somebody's trying to poison me!" Kevin shouted. "The food was meant for me, not Jermaine!"

Aghast, Emma tugged on his arm. *Chill, Kevin!*

Dr. Lindstrom's eyes widened, and she took another step backward. "I'll review his lab results, but as of now, I see no evidence Jermaine is suffering from anything other than ordinary food poisoning."

"Couldn't his stomach contents be examined for poisons?" Emma asked while trying to edge Kevin away. He ignored her and continued to glare at the physician.

"Or maybe other tests could be done?" Kelly tugged on Kevin's other arm.

"Jermaine vomited all his stomach contents," Dr. Lindstrom said, "and while I'll be glad to review his case, I don't order extra tests unless I see a clear indication they're needed."

"In other words, you're going to do exactly nothing!" Kevin shook Emma and Kelly loose and bellowed in the physician's face. "You don't care, do you?"

Dr. Lindstrom's weary face hardened. She stuck her phone to her ear. "Security?"

OK, I think we're done here. Though Kevin frightened Emma too, she joined forces with Kelly to drag him to the exit. As they left, Emma welcomed the glacial air that slapped her hot cheeks. She cast a glance over her shoulder. Would hospital security follow them to the parking garage?

They reached the Jeep without incident and sat in silence for a moment. Kevin hunched in the rear seat. "I suppose I should say I'm sorry."

She turned and looked him in the eye. "Are you?" *Not helpful, Emma.* She bit her lip.

Kevin raised his head. "I'm not sorry I asked more questions than she wanted to answer." Then his shoulders sagged again. "Maybe I could have ... said it differently."

If you hadn't lost it, she might have listened to you. To us.

"I'm glad Jermaine's going to be all right," Kelly said.

"I'll cover his hospital bill." Kevin, studying the Jeep's floor, spoke as if talking to himself. "I doubt he has insurance."

Kevin Crawford, you're either a caring man, or you're the best liar I've ever met. Emma steered the Jeep out of the garage and into raging evening traffic.

They pulled to a stop at a red light. A flash of new frustration erupted in Emma's already-roiling thoughts when she glanced into her rearview mirror. Kevin was not clutching his tea bottle.

He had forgotten it, and so had she.

fourteen

"Kevin, you're looking as skinny as this carrot stick." Dottie Faye waggled the julienned strip at him as she burst into his dressing room. Reed trailed after her, carrying her picnic basket. "You need to eat, or you're going to turn into nothing but a straight line with teeth."

Emma saw a small smile tease Kevin's lips. *Go, Dottie. That's the first smile I've seen on his face in days—other than on the stage.*

With the air of a conjurer, her aunt produced paper plates, lumberjack-sized ham sandwiches, and an enormous, gooey coconut cake from her basket. "It's nasty outside, but we can have a picnic in here. I brought Granny Murleen's Make-Him-Want-to-Marry-You Cake."

"Yes!" Herbie pumped his fist, and Kevin's smile widened. For once, both seemed to forget Reed's presence.

The cake—Dottie's one and only cooking specialty—did look delicious. Between her and Herbie, maybe they'd all shake their gloomies for awhile. To Emma, it seemed evil storms had taken up permanent residence in New York City. She, Dottie, and Kelly found trailing Madison and Landon during nonstop rain and sleet a tough assignment. Plus, they'd learned nothing new.

But sweet tea could raise even the most waterlogged spirits. Emma knew that between it and the huge chunk of cake Dottie always served, her metabolism would run on sugar power for the next twenty years. Today, she didn't care.

Kevin's dietary scruples didn't cross Emma's mind until Dottie Faye said, "Kevin, you won't disappoint me, will you?"

"I'm sorry, Dottie Faye." He looked genuinely apologetic. "I don't eat much meat, especially pork."

"I figured that." She uncovered a bowl of crisp green salad. "I bought those fancy greens and cheeses with names I can't pronounce. Have at it, son."

Kevin dug in. "This is really good. Thanks, Dottie Faye."

"But that's not all." Dottie Faye beamed. "I brought the biggest pepper grinder I could find. The bigger the grinder, the classier the salad, right?"

Before he could say a word, she cranked a blast of potent fresh pepper from a grinder that was more cannon than condiment holder. The pepper rained not only on Kevin's salad, but on everything and everyone else. Emma's eyes watered, and she joined in a chorus of "ahhhhhh-*choos!*"

"Dottie, maybe Kevin doesn't like pepper!" Kelly protested.

"Of course, he does. Don't you, darlin'?" Her aunt pulled a box of tissues from her basket. "Goodness, your allergies must be kicking up. Need one, Kevin?"

He'd covered his face with his handkerchief as if shielding himself from a plague. "No, thanks," he wheezed. "I need some air. I'll be back."

He left, despite her protests. While the others brushed off themselves and their sandwiches, Emma noted her aunt's disappointed little sigh. *Good try, Dottie Faye. But tissues? You'll never separate Kevin from his beloved handkerchief.*

Despite the pepper storm, the picnic resumed, and with it, some of the fun. Herbie teased Dottie about her gigantic grinder, and to Emma's surprise, Reed joined in. Kevin dared return to eat some of the salad that had escaped fallout. He even ate a slice of Granny Murleen's cake—but with a real fork he dug out of a drawer and rinsed immediately afterward, using organic soap.

Who would win the undeclared tug-of-war? Emma covered a grimace at Kevin's compulsiveness and a chuckle at Dottie's determination to collect his DNA.

Emma nearly swallowed her own fork, though, when her aunt, with a motherly smile, reached toward Kevin's mouth. "You got something between your teeth. Let me get it for you."

He clapped his hand over his mouth. "I'll take care of it," he mumbled. "I have to have my costume refitted anyway."

Later, as Emma, Kelly, and Dottie relaxed in their sitting room, Dottie fumed, "I'd swear that boy has caught on to my DNA hunt."

"I don't think so," Kelly soothed.

"I should just knock him into next Tuesday and scrape off his skin."

Shaking her head, Emma went to bed. At least Dottie came up with original ways to achieve their mission. And she never quit.

Unfortunately, neither could Emma's brain. Her pillow seemed full of gravel. At midnight, she rose, found her way to the kitchen, and opened the refrigerator. A large, luscious chunk of Granny Murleen's cake remained. Would it provide sufficient food for great thoughts?

Emma slid the box out of the fridge and prepared to find out.

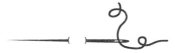

"Shall we their fond pageant see? Lord, what fools these mortals be!"

Emma had seen Kevin deliver those lines several times. During this scene rehearsal prompted by new lighting staff, boyish devilment sparkled in his eyes, undiminished by many performances.

As Oberon, the fairy king, responded with his lines, however, Kevin's expression waned. Or did it? Emma blinked. She must be imagining things.

It occurred again as Shakespeare's Greek lovers, bewitched by a love potion gone wrong, sang their hilarious song. Emma watched Kevin lose his focus, then recover. His delivery slowed as the scene continued. Now his mouth hung loosely, and his wonderful storytelling eyes went blank.

"What's wrong with Kevin?" Kelly whispered from her seat beside her.

"I don't know." Emma moved to the edge of her seat.

"Jack ... shall have Jill ..." Kevin's words slurred. He stared at the lights, groping for the next line.

"What's the matter? Are you all right?" The director sounded more annoyed than concerned.

"Nought shall ... go ill ..."

Kevin's mouth contorted. He toppled over.

Emma leaped to her feet and dashed down the aisle, Kelly at her heels, as the director ran up the stage steps. Greek lovers, fairies, and Nick Bottom wearing his donkey's head poured from the wings. The bizarre scene might have seemed funny, except that Kevin lay white as a corpse on the stage floor, barely moving.

A chorus member who worked part time as an EMT checked Kevin's pulse and shook his head. Brannigan barked the theater's address into his phone while the EMT loosened Kevin's clothes. Emma realized she was standing directly in front of the stage, in front of Kevin, her hand over her mouth.

Madison, wearing her filmy fairy garb, stood directly across from Emma, hand over her mouth too.

No paparazzi or autograph hounds here. Emma, sitting by Kelly, gave thanks the hospital had barred this small waiting room from the press and curiosity seekers.

"Have the doctors told you anything else?" Brannigan, so brash when directing, spoke in a subdued tone.

"No. Kevin's still unconscious," Reed answered. "They don't know if he'll come out of it or not."

Dottie Faye, her mascara intact despite tears, squeezed his arm.

"Kevin doesn't take sleeping pills!" Herbie leaped from his chair and spat the last words as if they were expletives. "He won't even take vitamins."

Kelly stood, stopped Herbie from pacing, and placed her hands on his shoulders. "Look, the doctor only told us Kevin's test results; he wasn't telling us how the sedative got into Kevin's system."

"I know." The teen dropped into a chair, his eyes moistening. "But Kevin would never OD on anything."

Several actors who had accompanied Brannigan murmured assent and tried to console Herbie, but they, too, appeared stunned.

While Kelly comforted the young man, Landon Green stared blankly along with the rest—until his gaze rested on Emma. He gaped as if trying to remember her. Her heartbeat jumped, but she gave him a disinterested glance that said, *I hang out at The Paddington.*

Landon returned to chatting with the others in the quiet, awkward conversations people have during a crisis. Emma exhaled. Evidently he didn't recognize her or Kelly from their stakeouts. She pretended to read a magazine, all the while studying his face and mannerisms. What part did he play in all this intrigue? She was tempted to ask him why Madison hadn't come too.

Enough about those two—for now. Emma turned her thoughts to Kevin. Whether he had overdosed voluntarily or not, whether he was linked to the killings, he himself was now fighting for his life. Emma stared through the waiting area across the hall at double doors that separated them from the drama within. She didn't know how to feel or what to think. She didn't know what to do.

So she sat in silence and prayed.

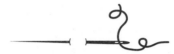

"Th-thanks." Kevin reached a feeble hand for Emma's.

She did not withdraw it. "I'm so sorry this happened, Kevin."

While machines blinked and blipped around him, he lay back on the hospital bed as if the single word had exhausted him. Unlike most ICU patients, Kevin's celebrity status had landed him a private room.

The gray hairs Dottie Faye had tried to pull seemed more noticeable here. No silver lit his grayish white eyes. Even his thin face looked gray. An IV linked to his arm, and tubes and wires clung to him like spiderwebs.

The hospital ordinarily would not have allowed Emma in the room, as they permitted only family to visit patients as sick as Kevin. But he had no family.

She hadn't wanted to come. She'd wanted to remain in the waiting room with the others, keeping eyes and ears open for clues as to how and why this had happened. But when Kevin asked for her, what else could she do?

Kevin's eyes closed, and she thought he had fallen asleep. Still she sat near the window, watching clouds drift freely in the sky, wishing she could cut loose too.

A strand of saliva ran out of Kevin's mouth. Emma's DNA alert went off.

If she dabbed his mouth oh so gently with a tissue, they'd have their sample.

I have to do this. If Kevin dies, our chance to collect his DNA will die with him.

She pulled a tissue from a box on his nightstand.

But the sight of his corpselike form, trussed with wires and tubes, halted her hand midair. How could she violate Kevin's personal rights when he lay so helpless, so near death? Especially if he were innocent of the murders.

Emma grappled half the night with her thoughts. Finally, she gave in to the rhythmic electronic music of the machines and fell asleep, sitting upright in the uncomfortable chair.

Kevin's voice startled her out of turbulent dreams of a man drowning in Mystic Harbor.

"I didn't," he said.

Though groggy, Emma understood. He wanted her to know he hadn't overdosed on the illegal sedative found in his blood, Rohypnol—"roofies" in the street vernacular.

He tried to raise his head. "I didn't!"

"I know." Whatever else about Kevin she didn't understand, Emma believed him now. The quiver of his colorless lips and burgeoning fear in his eyes confirmed what they both knew.

Someone else had wanted him dead. And that someone was still out there.

fifteen

"How's Kevin?" A curly-haired woman reporter nearly thrust a microphone into Emma's mouth as she, Kelly, and Dottie left the hospital. "Did he tell you why he overdosed?"

Dottie Faye had sulked because she couldn't visit Kevin, but now her nostrils flared. "Leave her alone!"

"Why don't you let her speak for herself?" the woman snapped back.

"No comment." Emma didn't make eye contact with her or with any of the other faces bobbing around her.

"He asked for you, didn't he?" another called while cameras clicked and whirred.

How did you know that?

"How long have you dated?"

"We're not dating." She wanted to plow through like a halfback.

"Right." Chuckles of derision. "Then how long have you known Kevin?"

Kelly's icy voice broke in. "Is this how you treat people in crisis? Very nice. I'll bet you spring for dinner when their friends actually die."

Silence for five seconds. Then more questions. Kelly took Emma's right arm, Dottie Faye her left, and they hurried away.

They almost jogged to the parking garage without speaking. When they reached the Jeep, Emma drew them to her. "Thank you. I couldn't handle those people today."

Kelly offered to drive, but Emma needed routine. As they sped from the hospital, Dottie Faye glowered at their foes. Some lingered outside the entrance, apparently hoping another of Kevin's visitors would appear. "I wish I had my old BB gun. I'd scatter that bunch of crows in no time."

Emma cast a smile over her shoulder. "Kelly, would you find the police station nearest the Theater District on your phone? We haven't had much luck with the Mystic Harbor police, but I think this precinct should know what's going on at The Paddington." She told them what Kevin had said.

Dottie Faye sniffed. "I already knew that."

"He's so careful about what he puts into his body. Sleeping pills? I don't think so." Kelly tapped her phone. "The police station's actually within walking distance of The Paddington."

The brick station resembled an old-movie counterpart, with long windows and an arched entrance. They entered a room filled with cluttered desks, clanking radiators, and people with complaints. A businesslike policewoman at the front desk, upon hearing they wanted to share information, told them she'd work them in.

More waiting. Emma hated it. But she'd wait all night if she had to.

When officers hauled in two combative women with glittery eyes, spouting profanity, Emma wondered if it would come to that.

To her surprise, a gray-haired, stocky officer soon called her name and gestured for them to follow him. Photos of towheaded kids—grandchildren?—adorned his chaotic desk. Perhaps this man had a heart. Emma hoped so.

He told them he was Detective Baines, dragged clunky old chairs to his desk for them, then leveled penetrating hazel eyes at Emma. "Names and addresses, please?"

They introduced themselves.

"From Massachusetts, huh? Vacationing in the Big Apple?"

"A combination of business and pleasure," Emma said. She and the others had decided beforehand not to mention their real mission. "We've been visiting the Garment District. Kelly and I own a quilting shop in Mystic Harbor."

"We're all members of the Nimble Thimbles." Dottie beamed.

Emma groaned inwardly. *Too much information, Dottie Faye.* Now, despite the complexity and art of their profession, the man would consider them lightweights.

"I see," he said. "How can I help you?"

Emma began with Brett Damon's death. The detective remembered the case. "That's a sad situation. We're still working on it, but nothing new has come up."

"Nothing about the doctor who took him away?" Emma asked.

"Nothing I can disclose outside of the department."

She'd expected as much. Keeping her tone level, Emma continued, "Brett was Kevin Crawford's understudy in the musical *A Midsummer Night's Dream*, which is playing at The Paddington. I'm sure you're already aware Kevin is now in the hospital with an alleged sedative overdose."

"I think all New York knows about that one," Baines said drily.

Emma took a deep breath. "We think whoever killed Brett Damon actually meant to kill Kevin Crawford. And that when the murderer failed the first time, he tried again."

Baines's expression changed little, but he leaned forward. "You have reason to believe this?"

Emma showed him photos of Brett and Kevin and pointed out how Brett's killer may have mistaken the understudy for the actor. She related how Brett's family and pastor insisted he had no enemies. They denied any connection between Brett and drugs or dealers.

Detective Baines scribbled notes on a yellow legal pad. "Anything else?"

"Plenty." With a few asides from Kelly and Dottie Faye, Emma described the pranks played on Kevin after Brett's death and how Herbie had heard Madison Leigh blame Kevin for hurting her career. Emma told him about Jermaine's food poisoning. Then she advised him of Kevin's denial in the hospital and his obsessive-compulsive habits that steered him far from pills of any kind.

Baines laid down his pen. "This is all very interesting, ladies. I appreciate your coming forward with the information."

Emma fumed, feeling that she had been dismissed. She measured her words. "I realize most of this is conjecture. We can't give you hard evidence. But taken all together, these clues point to a killer who will pursue his ends, no matter what." She wouldn't tell him about Rose, but she did inform him of the identity theft she and Kelly had endured and the parking-garage mugger.

Detective Baines tapped the pen on his desk. "And you believe these occurred because you and your friends have been investigating your suspicions on your own?"

"We've asked questions." Emma raised her chin.

For the first time, the man frowned slightly. "I appreciate your concern for Mr. Crawford, but if what you suspect is true, you may be placing yourself in danger—as well as complicating official investigations." He paused. "You are, according to the newspapers, a close friend of his?"

Emma flushed but tried to plane irritation from her voice. "They'll turn anything into a headline. We all are Kevin's friends."

"I see." Detective Baines sat silent for several minutes. Emma fidgeted. Much as she hated Tom Boyer's stonewalling, she found this policeman's inscrutability unsettling. Dottie Faye kept crossing and uncrossing her legs, a sure sign she soon would explode.

Finally, he spoke. "Coming from a small town, you probably see all these events at The Paddington as unusual. I understand why you think they're interrelated and that a single criminal must be behind them. But the truth is, our precinct sees this kind of thing frequently."

Emma bristled. "One death, one near-death, and a food poisoning in one show's cast, all within a month? That hardly seems coincidental."

Baines nodded. "A bit more than usual—but still not abnormal, given the circumstances—"

"Which are?" Emma crossed her arms.

Baines crossed his too. "First, Brett Damon seemed squeaky clean at the time of his death, but his doctor says that as a teen, he had a bad car accident and got hooked on painkillers."

Emma inhaled sharply. Brett's pastor, in his refusal to discuss the actor's past, had implied something like that. Baines went on, "He got off those at a pain clinic, but Brett may have suffered a relapse. No record of his going to a clinic recently. Instead, he may have initiated contact with some nasty people. I don't know what he did to make them kidnap him in broad daylight, but these guys have a real talent for their own kind of drama." His lips pressed together in a grim smile.

Emma ached to tell him about Rose and Mystic Harbor's small-town drama, but she held her tongue. "And Kevin?"

His craggy face softened. "He may not have told you, but Crawford used drugs extensively as a young man."

The officer's fatherly expression told Emma he still believed she was Kevin's girlfriend. She said briskly, "I'm not surprised. But he's shown no recent evidence of that—"

"He hasn't?" Baines picked up a folder and read. "'Agent, director, and fellow actors all say Kevin Crawford has exhibited wide mood swings lately, extreme irritability, irrationality, and increasing paranoia, with a shrinking appetite and great difficulty sleeping.'" He looked her in the eye. "Classic user symptoms."

Emma battled her impulse to shout a retort.

But Dottie Faye had no such scruples. "That boy's not taking anything! He's just not quite right in the head!" she yelled, loud enough so faces all over the room popped up and swiveled their way.

Thank you, Dottie Faye. Emma closed her eyes.

"We often deal with actors." Baines's maddeningly reasonable voice took control again. "Artistic people live under extreme pressure. Drugs, emotional struggles, intergroup tensions and jealousies—those would explain the goings-on at The Paddington."

"And Jermaine's poisoning?" Now Emma didn't bother to lower her voice.

"Do you have any idea how many people in New York get sick on takeout?" He shrugged. "Not a wise move on Crawford's part to accept a meal from an unknown source, and even worse to give it to a friend. I hope he's learned his lesson."

Drip ... drip ... drip ... The man's benign logic wore on Emma like Chinese water torture. "So you're going to do nothing."

"I didn't say that." Those level hazel eyes again.

Emma looked away. "If we're right, Kevin is still in danger."

"He's in a hospital, not a dark alley."

"Brett wasn't in a dark alley, either."

The detective sighed. "I'll talk with the hospital security and have them check on Crawford several times a day. Given his celebrity status, they probably already are. And I'll check on him daily too." He leaned forward. "I don't discount your information, Ms. Cotton. But you must understand that we have to look at these cases in context. Like I said, we see a lot of these situations."

Emma wanted to beat on his desk with both fists. Instead, she clenched them in her lap and forced a smile. "Thanks, anyway."

"I will keep what you've said in mind." He stood.

What a waste of time. Emma and the others rose.

Baines guided them toward the door. "I assume you plan to continue your investigations." A statement, not a question.

"Yes." Kelly spoke up. "We believe Kevin needs us."

"I know you do." His riveting gaze stopped Emma mid-step. "You must be very careful."

Translation: "I don't believe you—but be careful." I am so tired of this. Emma nodded curtly and walked with Kelly and Dottie Faye out the door.

"He does make good points," Kelly said.

"I still think he's wrong," Emma snapped.

"Dead wrong." Dottie nodded. "But he's nice. Kind of cute too, and so polite. I wonder if he's from the South."

Emma knew where this was leading. "Please, not another word, Dottie Faye Sinclair. Not another word."

"Oh, all right." Dottie had to have the last word. At least she left it at that.

"Do you want me to drive now?" Kelly held out her hand for Emma's keys.

She handed them over. "Yes. But drop me off at the hospital."

"The hospital?" Kelly raised an eyebrow. "They may not let you see Kevin again today."

"You already got to see him," Dottie Faye grumbled.

"Fine," Emma said. "You take the first shift, if you want. I'll go home and sleep."

"Shift? What are you talking about?" her aunt demanded. Kelly wrinkled her nose.

"Exactly what I said." Emma climbed into the Jeep's backseat. "A few security guards checking on Kevin during their coffee breaks won't deter a criminal who's killed once and attempted it twice more." She raised her chin. "We might not be allowed to visit, but we can watch from the waiting area to see who enters his room. And that's what I intend to do."

sixteen

"Why won't they let me see Kevin?" Dottie whined like a nine-year-old. But she'd earned some latitude. Her eight-hour shift of monitoring Kevin had just ended, and even her perfect makeup couldn't disguise dark circles under her eyes. "I just sit here in this boring old waiting room. Even the reporters won't talk to me anymore. They always want you."

"Well, I don't want them." Emma had chosen to begin her shift at midnight, when she could guard their celebrity in relative peace. "And I'd be glad to let you take my place with Kevin."

So far, the doctors had severely limited visitation, only allowing Emma and Reed for short periods. Kevin still looked gray and emaciated, like a hoary phantom from a Shakespearean tragedy.

"You've been so faithful in helping your friend." Dottie wrapped her arm around Emma. "You aren't falling for Kevin, are you, sweet pea?"

"No." Emma yawned. "Just trying to keep him alive."

She hustled her aunt into the elevator and returned to the waiting room, all the while keeping one eye trained on Kevin's room. Guilt niggled at her. *You could collect his DNA in a second. Do it.*

Yes, she could play the part of an angel of mercy, swabbing Kevin's mouth while he slept.

No. Not with him so ... defenseless.

Even if he's a murderer?

Thankfully, a nurse interrupted Emma's thoughts with a pleasant greeting. Emma returned the wave, though the knowing smile on the woman's face made Emma want to yell, "He's not my boyfriend! OK?"

Fortunately, the nurses kept too busy to pry, but when Kevin asked for her and clutched her hand, Emma could count on a dozen sappy looks.

Shaking off the thought, she sipped espresso and peered down the long hallway where Kevin's room was located. How had his attacker infused roofies into his system? According to Emma's research, Rohypnol, a tasteless, colorless sedative, could easily be slipped into a drink. But Kevin carried his water bottle at all times.

Brett was injected with ketamine, a different sedative. Could Kevin's would-be murderer have injected him too?

But the hospital doctors had said Kevin ingested the medication.

Was his water bottle with him when he collapsed? Emma couldn't recall. The thing seemed like his Siamese twin ... except during performances. Maybe someone had slipped the Rohypnol into his bottle the night before when he was onstage. But Kevin, lately consumed with fear, always locked his dressing room.

Even if he had forgotten and the assailant had succeeded in tainting his water, symptoms would have appeared much earlier. According to Emma's research, Rohypnol symptoms occurred as quickly as twenty minutes after ingestion. Kevin's illness hadn't begun until the next afternoon.

Did he take the Rohypnol himself?

Emma shook her head. Overdosing just didn't fit Kevin. Perhaps the culprit concealed it in his food? But Kevin, who spent most of that day at The Paddington, refused to eat out after Jermaine's incident and no longer brought food to eat in private. He'd even given up soy nuts. His daily fasts along with the timing of the onset of his symptoms made the drugged-food alternative nearly impossible.

As she thought of how little Kevin ate, Emma heard Detective Baines review users' symptoms, including loss of appetite. Kevin's youthful history of drug abuse nagged at her.

No. He didn't take roofies voluntarily. Her gut couldn't accept it.

A nearby elevator *zzwooped* open. Emma jumped. She'd been thinking more than watching.

A security guy in his navy uniform exited the elevator. *Dan Greeson.* Emma's tight muscles relaxed. He was a huge fan of Kevin's and considered protecting him a privilege. Dan waved, walked down the long hall, and entered Kevin's room.

Emma made a mental note to thank Baines for keeping his promise to work with hospital security. During her watches, she'd seen officers checking on Kevin.

Emma scanned the hallway, admonishing herself to be more watchful. No big, scary criminals would encroach on her turf.

But what if the killer—or killers—weren't big and scary? The distinguished-looking "doctor" who had tended Brett had epitomized a caring physician. She should look out for that type. She also thought of Madison, fragile and lovely in her fairy costume—perhaps an exotic, deadly femme fatale. Emma wished they could continue monitoring her movements as closely as they had.

She rechecked the Mace in her bag and riveted her gaze on Kevin's door.

If the fairy had murder on her mind, she'd need more than pixie dust to make it past Emma.

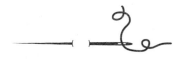

During the next night's guard duty, Emma debated whether to ask Kevin about his water bottle. She had no business poking around in his belongings without permission. But he was weak—so frail that he hadn't even fussed about it. If his water bottle were missing, she, Kelly, and Dottie Faye needed to locate it immediately. If it didn't turn up at The Paddington or his apartment—she'd check if Herbie or Reed had access—she would report its absence to Baines. Surely, though, Kevin's assailant would have destroyed it.

Emma *had* to find out if that water bottle had accompanied Kevin to the hospital.

A nurse wearing a French braid and a wide smile approached Emma, the signal that Kevin had awakened and wanted her to join him.

Did she hear fewer blips and beeps as she entered the room? Perhaps a slight tinge of color touched his face?

Kevin reached for her hand. "Hey."

"Hey. You feeling better?" She didn't possess the most entertaining bedside manner, but Kevin didn't seem to expect brilliant conversation.

He smiled wanly. "Reed came."

"I'll bet they miss you at The Paddington."

Kevin closed his eyes. "Not like I miss the show."

"I don't blame you. I hate …" Emma caught herself, but he finished her sentence.

"You hate hospitals too?"

She flushed. "Um."

"Thanks for sticking with me."

"We want to keep you safe." She wished he wouldn't cling to her hand. When Kevin fell asleep, she'd gently withdraw it. As he improved, surely he'd realize she wouldn't hold his hand for the next twenty years.

Kevin dozed off. Emma waited until his breathing length-ened into long, rhythmic patterns, then slipped away. He shifted, but continued to sleep. She forced herself to wait another ten minutes, then padded softly to the nurses' check-list at the door. Hospitals and privacy were opposites. The nurse had seen Kevin less than a half hour ago, yet that did not guarantee that she, a doctor, or security guard would not charge in at any moment.

Emma couldn't wait any longer. Praying for no squeaks, she crept to the closet and slowly swung the door open. So far, so good. She flicked on a tiny flashlight and scanned the closet shelves, its floor. A glimmer answered its light. Emma leaned forward. The water bottle! Kevin had carried it when he collapsed. She reached for it.

"I thought of that too."

Her blood iced, then heated. Still facing away from Kevin, Emma said, "I should have asked you before searching your things. I'm sorry."

"Looking out for me, are you?"

She made herself turn around. A ghost of Kevin's Puckish persona greeted her, which unsettled her more than his anger would have. "So you were carrying your water bottle when you got sick."

"Yes. Always keep it with me. I watch my things. Did I eat? No. Don't eat until after the show." The glitter in his eyes, though subdued, made hairs prickle on her neck. "So you think I OD'd too?" he asked.

"Not voluntarily." Emma closed the closet door. "Given your personality, your habits, it doesn't make sense."

To her amazement, he chuckled faintly. "'Doesn't make sense.' Love it. Love that about you. Sensible Emma."

His eyes faded to pewter once more, and he dropped on his pillow. "Sit by me?"

She wanted to run. Instead, she sat.

She let Kevin clasp her hand, and he fell into a deep sleep. Emma sneaked away to the waiting room, and, like a sentinel, took her position across from the elevator. Between Kevin's brief periods of wakefulness, she pondered and paced away the long, long night.

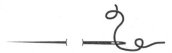

It was only a half hour before Kelly would show up. Emma watched the inflow and outflow of nurses and aides as they changed shifts. After Kevin had caught her searching his closet last night, Emma couldn't wait to leave. She'd work out in Lucinda's mini-gym before she crashed, then figure things out later.

At the far end of the dim hallway, a red-haired nurse wearing the traditional white cap caught Emma's eye. Few nurses wore them anymore. The woman carried an enormous stack of bedsheets, obscuring her face. She whisked into a room. Emma turned her attention elsewhere in the awakening hallway, but left a bit of her focus, like a safety light, on that room's door.

She waited.

No nurse exited.

From what Emma had observed, morning nurses zipped around, executing endless to-do lists. Most stayed only a few minutes in a room. At seven o'clock, Emma couldn't imagine they gave baths. What kept the nurse in that room so long?

Red hair ... Madison. The nurse appeared taller than Kevin's ex-girlfriend, and if she planned to do him in, why would she have stopped—for a long time—in another room?

Or perhaps the woman was the female murderer from Rose's class?

"Anything happen last night?"

At Kelly's voice, Emma jumped, but she kept her eyes on the door. "Yeah, but let's talk about that later. Right now, I'm not sure what's happening." She told Kelly about the redhead.

"That's odd."

The frown in her partner's voice reassured Emma. She stood, hung her bag on her shoulder, and reached in for her can of Mace. "This may be nothing. But I think we should ..."

At that moment, the nurse with the cap emerged. She walked toward Kevin's room.

Ducking people and carts, Emma and Kelly strode down the hall and directly into the red-haired nurse's path.

"Could you help me, ma'am?" Emma's fingers tightened on the Mace. "We're here to visit Kevin Crawford."

The woman did an about-face, but Emma and Kelly, on either side, clasped her arms firmly.

They then dropped them. Emma's jaw dropped too.

"Y'all don't have to grab so hard," Dottie Faye sniffed. "I'll turn black and blue."

Tremors began in Emma's tired, twisted stomach and swelled into an earthquake. Kelly stood between them. "Let's go to the waiting room and talk."

"Let me put these sheets somewhere." Another reproachful look from Dottie. "They're awfully heavy."

"I'll buy us coffee," Emma said, glancing at Kelly. *If you'll keep an eye on the criminals.* Kelly nodded.

Emma started toward the elevator, continuing to navigate around busy personnel and equipment. *That's why Dottie came so early.* Her aunt knew she could blend into the morning rush with little chance of being discovered.

Before Emma left the floor, she entered an empty patient room, closed the door, and pounded the daylights out of a pillow. She emerged somewhat refreshed and bought coffee.

As Emma entered the waiting room, her annoyance lessened a little. Dottie no longer wore the cap—though she still wore the wig and a crisp white uniform that flattered her long legs.

The few early visitors apparently had left for breakfast. The nurses and other staff looked too busy to listen to their discussion. *No witnesses. That's good.* Emma handed Kelly her latte. "Would you mind watching Kevin's room while we talk?" *And keep me from killing my aunt?*

"No problem." Kelly shifted so she could supervise all.

Emma gave Dottie her coffee, sat beside her, and said carefully, "Would you please explain this masquerade?"

"Masquerade?" Dottie's eyebrows arched. "I think of it as acting. I always have been quite the thespian, you know. No one knew I wasn't a nurse until you two hauled me off like the Gestapo."

"Do you realize you could be arrested for impersonating a nurse?" Kelly asked. "If someone had discovered you before we did, we'd be raising your bail right now."

"I only wanted to see Kevin." Dottie swapped the haughty Southern belle for an innocent blue-eyed child.

Emma kept an iron grip on her words. "Kevin's feeling better. I imagine his doctors will lift the visitor restrictions soon."

"I should hope so. So silly," Dottie Faye grumbled. "I could do a better job than half the nurses in this hospital."

Emma wanted to bury her face in her hands. "I suppose you walked up the stairs, since I didn't see you on the elevator. Then you stayed forever in that room at the other end. Why?"

"I met the sweetest little old man. He'd been in the hospital so long." Dottie brightened. "I gave him a foot rub."

"A foot rub?" Tiny tremors shook Emma again, but this time she realized they were chuckles.

Kelly giggled too. "I imagine you added ten years to his life?"

"Darn tootin'." Dottie Faye shook her red locks. "We had fun, and by the time I left, he was laughing like a kid. I could work miracles on this floor if they would just turn me loose."

Picturing that, Emma closed her eyes again. But her aunt was right. Sort of. She did bring joy into people's lives with her passion for life, her generosity, and her incredible sense of fun. Dottie overdid it when she spread her sunshine, and people near her were likely to suffer sunburns. But no one could stay gloomy with Dottie Faye around.

Emma slipped an arm around her aunt. "You do help lots of people. I know you want to help Kevin."

"I just think we can protect him better if we stick with him." Dottie slapped the sofa arm for emphasis.

Again, her aunt had a point. Emma couldn't imagine any aggressor surviving a bedpan attack.

"When Kevin feels he can handle more company, I'll ask him to talk to his doctors," Emma assured her. "In the meantime, will you agree not to play nurse again?"

Dottie Faye pouted. "Oh, all right. But I hate to waste this lovely outfit." She yawned. "I'll just have to think of some other way to use it."

Emma blotted the possibilities from her mind. "We have something else we need to discuss. Kevin's hospitalization presents the perfect opportunity to harvest his DNA."

"It does, doesn't it?" Dottie Faye's eyes lit up. "Paper cups, tissues, swabs—"

"I could have collected a half dozen samples by now." Emma looked them in the eye. "But I couldn't."

No one said anything for a moment.

"I guess we haven't thought much about DNA since Kevin was brought here." Kelly leaned her head on her hand. "We've just been hoping he'd survive."

"He's still so pitiful he probably can't spit without help," Dottie said.

"But how long do we wait? Till Kevin's out of the hospital? Finished with therapy? Well-adjusted? I don't think so." Emma crossed her arms. "He seemed better last night. If Kevin's stable tonight—the night shift's when we risk less interruption—I'll collect the sample." She set her jaw. "We have to do this for Rose."

"We can't forget what brought us here," Kelly agreed.

"Time for action." Dottie Faye stood and brushed a wrinkle from her uniform, a gleam in her eye.

"Oh no you don't." Emma rose and grasped her arm.

"But it would be so easy," Dottie pleaded, a grin spreading across her face. "I'd just walk into Kevin's room—"

"And run into a real nurse." Kelly shook her head. "I think you know that's not a good idea."

"You girls are never any fun."

"Sure we are." Emma pulled her aunt into a hug. "Did you have breakfast? They make amazing cream-cheese-stuffed French toast in the cafeteria. My treat."

"Don't torture me," Kelly groaned.

"I'll bring you some first," Emma promised. She turned to Dottie Faye. "Let's eat, then we'll catch up on our beauty sleep."

"Works for me." Dottie Faye yawned so hugely that her face morphed into one open lipsticked mouth. "I'm glad my shift doesn't start till afternoon. Why do all these people get up so early? It's downright unhealthy."

seventeen

"*K*evin *Crawford won't live long. Ditch him, or you won't either.*"

Emma, sitting in her room at Lucinda's, stared at her business email on her laptop. Tingles of terror and joy chased away her bleariness after only a few hours of sleep.

So much for Kevin's self-inflicted overdose. She decided not to wake Dottie, who was still snoozing after her early morning adventure. Emma did call Kelly, still doing guard duty at the hospital.

"The creep! He sent them to me too." Her partner sounded even angrier than when the identity thief had robbed them.

"But don't you see?" Emma hugged herself. "Kevin didn't OD. He didn't try to commit suicide. These emails shout that someone is trying to kill him."

"And they're after us."

"Well, that too." Emma's elation waned. "But this is something tangible we can report to Detective Baines. If the emails convince him Kevin truly is in danger, he might provide protection so we don't have to spend every minute on Kevin patrol."

"We need a break," Kelly agreed. "In the meantime, do you want me to call the Mystic Harbor police too?"

"I'd be forever grateful. After my last session with Boyer, he might hang up on me."

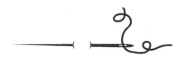

The threatening emails did raise Baines's eyebrows. He agreed to follow up on them and tested Emma's patience by warning her to "stay safe"—lock her lodgings and car; scrutinize online accounts, transactions, and social networks with even more care; avoid suspicious strangers; and stay home at night.

Right. She'd take reasonable precautions, but no way would Emma let him lock her in a cage. After the safety lecture, however, Baines told her he planned to interview Kevin, and if everything panned out, he would provide an officer outside Kevin's room 24/7.

She stopped by the Third Avenue Community Café.

"Good news?" Pastor Sam Dillinger grinned as he served her.

"I can breathe now." Stirring her mocha latte with double whipped cream, Emma updated him and related Baines's affirmation of their concerns.

Sam shook his head. "No wonder God has brought you to mind. I've prayed Brett's killer would be brought to justice. But I've also prayed for you and your friends every day."

"Thanks. We're still facing a lot." Separated from their own pastor and church, the Thimbles, their home—sometimes Emma had felt as if they fought this battle alone. Pastor Sam reminded her that they didn't.

Before returning to the café's counter, Sam told her that Brett's family was grieving but coping. More than ever, Emma hoped she and Kelly could unsnarl the painful mystery that obscured the case.

Right now, though, they needed to concentrate on Kevin's safety. *We should talk to Kevin about the emails too, before Baines calls him.*

Emma hated returning to the hospital early, but she felt as if an iron chain had been removed from her neck. An odd reaction. Death threats generally didn't make a person feel better. Emma's worries shrank, though, in that for the first time, someone took her and Kelly seriously.

"Why, Emma Jane. What are you doing here?"

Waiting for the elevator, Emma jumped at the familiar voice. "Hi, Dottie Faye." She hadn't realized it was time for her aunt's shift.

"You look tired." Dottie gave her a searching look. "Did you sleep? Why aren't you home in bed?"

"I saw Detective Baines, and I need to talk to Kevin." Saying it reminded her that she and Kelly would have to tell Dottie Faye about the emails too. Emma's optimistic mood flagged as they rode to Kevin's floor.

Kelly waved to them from the waiting room. "The nurses just told me Kevin can have more visitors now."

"Wonderful." Dottie Faye strode down the hall so fast even Emma had trouble keeping up with her.

So much for Emma's plan to discuss the email threats privately.

Kevin did look better. He still clutched Emma's hand while they chatted. She slipped it away when he took drinks from his water bottle, now placed on his night table.

She summoned her courage and said, "Kevin, you need to know about some emails Kelly and I received today."

Dottie's penciled eyebrows rose. "What kind of emails, sweet pea?"

"Well ... anonymous ones that threatened Kevin—and us as well if we continue to help him."

Fear slithered across Kevin's face. Dottie's turned purple, and she clenched her fist. "How dare that scum bully my niece again!" she yelled. "I'll find him and yank his hair out one strand at a time! I'll feed him to the rattlesnakes. I'll ..." She continued with every malediction the South had to offer.

Kevin's eyes widened, but by the time Dottie paused for breath, initial alarm had faded from his eyes, and a tiny grin tugged at his mouth.

Emma hugged her. "We'll be all right, Dottie Faye. Really. We discussed it with Detective Baines, and he actually plans to contact Kevin and discuss some protective measures."

"Thank you," was all Kevin said, but the same relief Emma had experienced buoyed his words. However, his earlier energy had faded. Kevin didn't need a relapse the first day he was allowed visitors, so Emma tugged gently on her aunt's elbow. "Kevin could use a nap. Let's go to the waiting room awhile, shall we?"

He gave her a grateful glance.

"Goodness gracious sakes," Dottie spewed, "someone is after this man! Anybody could walk in here while we're down the hall yakking and do him in."

Emma wanted to duct-tape her aunt's mouth.

"No siree." Dottie plopped her hands on her hips. "I stayed away when they made me, but now I'm not leaving until the police come."

With a resigned look, Kevin reached for his water bottle and tipped it up. Emma frowned.

"Are you thirsty?" Kevin asked, gazing at her curiously. "You're staring at my bottle."

"No ... that thin ring of red around the bottom—"

"What ring of red?" He eyed it.

"Not on the cylinder—on the bottom. Yours doesn't have that tiny red stripe." Emma took it from him and held it above them. Her heart began to thud. "Kevin, this isn't your bottle."

He stared at her, his mouth open, then grabbed it. "The scratch from when I dropped it in the parking lot—it's not there." He flung the bottle away as if it were radioactive. It clanged as it hit the floor and rolled away.

"Don't touch it, Dottie!" Emma cried as her aunt automatically bent to retrieve it. "It might still have the creep's fingerprints on it."

"Back at the theater, I rinsed the bottle after I drank from it," Kevin said, more pale than ever. "If someone had slipped something into it then, I would have washed it away."

Emma went limp with relief, as did the others. Kevin probably had destroyed any residue of the Rohypnol—and, unfortunately, any fingerprints. Still, they'd give the bottle to Baines for testing.

"I thought someone had it in for me, but this doesn't leave much doubt, does it?"

Kevin lay back on his pillow, eyes closed, chest rising and falling. His hand reached for Emma's, squeezing so hard she winced. Dottie moved her chair to the other side of his bed and took his other hand. Emma waited until Kevin's breathing quieted. The death grip on her hand relaxed, and she slipped her hand back to her lap.

Before she charged off to talk to Baines again, Kevin needed to recall his actions that day. And they needed to listen.

You can't go to sleep. Not yet. Emma said softly, "I know you don't feel like talking about this—"

He kept his eyes shut. "You've got that right."

"Emma Jane, stop pushing on him." Her aunt glared at her. "Can't you see he's had a shock? And whoever tried to kill him is still out there."

Kelly spoke to Kevin rather than Dottie. "We've already lost a lot of time. The sooner we nail down moments when someone could have drugged your water, the faster we'll find answers."

Silence. Then Kevin shifted to his side and opened his eyes. "OK."

"Think, Kevin. Who could have changed bottles on you?

Did anyone handle it, fill it for you?" Even as she asked, Emma pushed away one answer. *Not Herbie. Please, not Herbie.*

"No." He seemed to read her thoughts. "Herbie makes coffee, but I don't let anyone handle my water bottle."

"Did you leave it where maintenance or construction workers could grab it?" Kelly asked. "Costumers or dressers? Stagehands?"

Emma prodded her own brain. "This person could have paid someone to do it."

Kevin shook his head. "I wore my bottle on my belt. I always do, except during performances."

Emma knew he'd misinterpret her next question, but she had to know. "Did Madison Leigh have access to your water bottle?"

His face froze. For a moment, he said nothing. Then his words tripped over each other. "I suppose, since you asked, that you know we have a history together. But that was years ago." His eyes begged her to believe him.

Emma squirmed inwardly. *Look, I'm not interested in your love life.* She sighed, "I believe you."

Relief flooded his face. "Thank you. I wish Madison and I weren't in the same show, but that's life in theater." He shrugged. "Most of the time she's a professional. Occasionally she's a pain. Madison sometimes blows up about nothing. But I don't think she means anything by it."

Kelly gave Emma a reprieve from his intensity by grabbing the conversation. "Did you talk to her the day you became ill?"

He frowned. "She griped at me once that week—was it that day or the day before?—because she said my stage blocking in the first fairy scene hid the other actors' faces. Which meant, of course, that she thought I was upstaging her." Kevin rolled his eyes. "I told her what she already knew, that Brannigan makes those decisions. She fussed about something else. I don't remember what. But she didn't touch my bottle. It was hanging from my belt, like I said."

"When you drank from it, did you put it down for a moment?" Kelly leaned forward.

Emma couldn't help jumping in. "Did you drink while you talked to her?"

He fell back on his pillow with a groan. "I have no idea. But if she'd tried to grab it, I would have noticed."

Emma hated to badger him, and her aunt's pursed lips said that Dottie Faye would haul her to the woodshed if she kept tormenting the poor, sick boy. "Do you recall where you were when she approached you?"

"We were hanging out in the break area."

Emma shuddered. The same break area from which Brett had disappeared.

"Everybody was standing around." Kevin beat a clenched fist softly against the bed. "Actors, stagehands, Herbie, Brannigan. If I put the bottle down for a few seconds, anyone could have switched it—not just there, but anywhere else in the theater."

Anyone. Anywhere. Emma wanted to mash the stupid bottle flat. Instead, she patted Kevin's shoulder. "Thanks. That helps us know what we're dealing with. All right if I take this bottle to the police?"

Eyes shut again, he nodded. Emma pulled a paper bag from her purse. She donned a medical glove from a box near the sink and gingerly placed the bottle in the bag. "I'm sure most of the evidence has been washed away, but you never can tell."

"Just take it away." Kevin's color hadn't returned. Dottie Faye aimed an arrow of a look at Emma—until, catching her eye, light dawned on her aunt's face.

Emma knew Dottie Faye understood what she and Kelly already had grasped.

Kevin had just given her the perfect opportunity to get his fresh DNA.

"See you later." Emma walked toward the door. Kelly slipped her a Q-tip she'd quietly procured from a supply drawer. Emma hurried out, her heart pounding.

With luck, they'd latch onto evidence that pointed to Kevin's assailant.

Or maybe the bottle would implicate Kevin as the man who murdered Rose.

eighteen

"Times Square is awesome." Kelly blinked at the neon light show that lit the December dusk. "This was a great idea. Did you have a special reason for coming here?"

"No. I just asked myself, 'What's the opposite of a hospital?'" Emma gloried in their new freedom since Baines had posted the promised policeman outside Kevin's room. The huge "jumbotron" advertising displays flashed color and action on every side. The enormous Coca-Cola sign she'd seen on television dazzled her. News tickers, including the famous Dow Jones feed, glittered on numerous buildings, all of which illuminated the way for thousands of pedestrians. "Look, there's the Times Tower."

Kelly made a wry face. "Patrick never wants to go anywhere on New Year's Eve, so we watch the ball drop on TV." She held up her phone and clicked several photos. "Maybe these will convince him to spend one New Year's Eve here."

They oohed and aahed as they made their way through the Great White Way, the only neighborhood in Manhattan in which zoning laws *require* lighted signs. Usually Emma preferred simple pleasures. But tonight she inhaled the excitement that permeated Times Square and Broadway. She refused to think any more about the DNA she'd sent by overnight courier to Genetix International, Dottie Faye's quickie lab, which would send her results within a day or so. She pulled her mind away from the police's forensic tests on the water bottle. Today Emma wanted nothing more than to sample the best of the Big Apple with her best friend.

Her phone vibrated. She winced.

Kelly frowned. "Kevin again?"

"Voice mail is a wonderful invention." Since Emma had stopped spending hours at the hospital, he'd called her constantly. "Let's forget everything and have some fun."

She basked in New York City's magic, ran it over her tongue, and absorbed it through her pores. She savored the invisibility the crowd afforded. For the first time in weeks, Emma lost the "followed" feeling as they explored and window-shopped. How could a person—even one weighed down by a million concerns—stay glum when M&M's World loomed before them? Inside the store, dozens of devotees clustered around a two-story, fifty-foot-wide wall of tubes filled with thousands upon thousands of chocolate candies of every color and flavor. Emma had eaten peanut butter and pretzel M&M's, but these included mint, rice crisp, coconut, raspberry, and more!

Kelly's mouth hung agape. "I used to have dreams like this as a kid," she said reverently.

"Down, girl. It's December, remember?" Emma patted her own waistline. "I don't need those, and even you might think twice."

Kelly snorted, but before they could argue the point, a giant blue M&M character grabbed their hands.

All thoughts of dieting vanished. "You're my favorite," Emma told him. "I think I'll fill a bag with all blue M&M's."

"Me too." Kelly patted his face. He tugged at her arm. "Hey, where are we going?"

The M&M, apparently flattered, pulled them into an impromptu dance line. Children, teens, parents, and two gray-haired couples joined in dancing to the golden oldie "Sugar, Sugar." Emma stomped, turned, and clapped while other shoppers cheered. Maybe New York wasn't so grim after all.

The big M&M bowed to them afterward. They waved

goodbye and within minutes, obtained bags of multicolored dark chocolate candies bearing the words "Nimble Thimbles" for their friends. Kelly customized bags for Patrick, Keith, and Julie for Christmas and birthdays, but she stuffed several "for personal emergencies," as she told Emma.

Emma filled one with blue coconut M&M's for herself and pink, white, and lavender raspberry mixes for Dottie Faye and Lucinda.

The "personal emergency" idea made sense. Emma filled a second bag with all blues, this time with mixed flavors. She promised herself that whenever she couldn't take one more step of faith, she'd pop a few into her mouth and remember the night she had danced.

Emma and Kelly lost count of the shops they visited. Eventually they found their way to the Bubba Gump Shrimp Company. They'd focused on frugality since the identity theft disaster, so they split a big crab-stuffed shrimp appetizer.

As they waited for their order, Emma clicked her tongue in dismay. How could she have let M&M's World cast such a spell over her? "I can't believe I bought all this."

"You're giving most of it away, remember? To the Nimble Thimbles, Lucinda, and Dottie Faye," Kelly consoled her.

"Maybe these will sweeten up Dottie Faye—she's been temperamental lately." Emma shook her head. "I keep telling her marriage isn't on my bucket list, but she nags me to snap up Eric Hart. I have all but posted on a billboard that I am *not* interested in Kevin. Yet she practically points her BB gun at me whenever I visit him."

Kelly gave her a sympathetic look. "She knows he's in love with you."

Hot words leaped to Emma's lips, but she knew none of them were true. An exasperated sigh slipped out. "OK, OK, he's attached to me. It happens when a crisis throws people together."

"He's in love. Check your phone messages."

Clicking her tongue, Emma did. "Six. But that's just because he's obsessive."

"We're not talking about tissues versus hankies here, Emma." Kelly crossed her arms. "Look me in the eye and tell me I'm wrong."

Emma gripped her head. "What was I supposed to do?" The diners around them turned to stare. She sank her face into her hand and muttered, "The guy nearly died. Maybe I should have said, 'No, you can't hold my hand. You have to die by yourself'?"

"You didn't have a choice," Kelly patted her hand. "I would have done the same thing."

"But Kevin needs to know that I don't care for him like that. Even discounting the Rose thing, I couldn't think of him as more than a friend." She bit her lip. "I'll have to tell him. Soon."

So much for a carefree night. The platter of fragrant stuffed shrimp the waiter brought didn't look nearly as yummy.

"I'm sorry." Kelly grimaced. "I should have waited until after tonight to bring it up. But Kevin is obviously head over heels for you and falling deeper every day. I know it. Dottie Faye knows it. The entire hospital knows it. You, on the other hand, seem oblivious."

"I'm just not interested." A headache, an unwelcome guest, tapped at Emma's temples. "How do I approach him?"

"Have some shrimp while they're hot." Kelly never saw a situation that couldn't be helped by a great snack.

Emma's appetite had shrunk. "How are we supposed to handle Dottie? She declares that Kevin's all wrong for me but refuses to believe I agree with her."

Kelly paused mid-munch. "Do you think she herself has a May-December thing going?"

"A what?" Emma forgot about the shrimp.

"It happens." Kelly calmly dipped another shrimp in the restaurant's signature cocktail sauce. "Lately, Dottie Faye's hardly left Kevin's side, despite police protection. Reed's tried to talk her into dinner out, with no luck."

"I don't think so." Her aunt often followed the dictates of her inner crazy, but underneath the blond beehive, Dottie's brain remained surprisingly astute. "She loves feeling needed, and I'm sure she enjoys the company of a charismatic, up-and-coming younger actor. But—"

"But what? I think she's jealous."

Emma ignored her. "Dottie Faye's begun talking to him about financially supporting his career again. She still believes he'll pave her way to stardom." Emma tried to laugh.

"That's part of it." Kelly chuckled too, but shook her head gently. "However, if that were the main issue, Dottie wouldn't turn down dinner invitations from an agent like Reed."

Emma stared at Kelly. Her headache morphed into a continuous parade roll of pain. "OK. Now we're really in a mess."

Her partner tried to soothe her. "Once you tell Kevin you don't love him, she'll back off."

Emma, picturing the scene, stared sadly at what remained of the shrimp. "Who knows? Whatever happens, it won't be fun."

She reached into a bag and popped a few blue coconut M&M's. A few more. And then a handful.

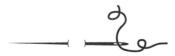

"I don't need to rest. You act as if I'm the one in the hospital bed." Dottie's anger spilled on Emma, Kelly, and Reed, who took her hand. "Why are you so worried all of a sudden that I can't handle it?"

Herbie's eyes widened as if afraid she'd take a swing at someone.

Kevin, lying on his pillows, threw Emma a weary look. Reed turned on the charm. "Dottie Faye, dear, you've taken such great care of my star. He left the ICU much sooner than anyone expected. He and I and his audience are forever in your debt."

The blue sparks in her aunt's eyes softened. "Kevin does look much better, doesn't he? But he's not out of the woods yet."

"Of course not," Reed crooned. "But spending a little time away won't hurt Kevin. Maybe dinner and a concert at the Rockefeller Center? I miss you, Dottie Faye."

Kelly, who, along with Herbie, had helped engineer this invitation, encircled Dottie's shoulders. "I'll stay with Kevin while you're gone."

"Or Emma can." Kevin reached for her hand.

Dottie's eyes sparked again. Emma wanted to clobber Kevin. Instead, she pulled her hand away and said, "Sorry, maybe later. I have plans this afternoon. In fact, I should leave right now."

Despite his frown, Emma left. She roamed to a far corner of the hospital for her "appointment" with a best-selling mystery. The book's plot probably wasn't as complicated as securing a private conversation with Kevin.

An hour later, her phone rang.

"It worked, Emma." Kelly spoke in hushed tones. "Until you left, I thought Reed would have to pry Dottie Faye away with a crowbar. But she left with him."

Emma exhaled. "Is Kevin asleep?"

"He zonked out. Sleep deprivation, I'm sure. The poor guy's probably had zero peace since she decided to play Florence Nightingale."

Emma fretted, "He can't sleep too long. What if Dottie Faye talks Reed into bringing her back early?"

"Let's give Kevin another hour. Then you come back, and we'll wake him. Gently, of course."

"Yeah, right." Emma hung up and fell back into her chair. They'd wake him gently, and then she'd blast him with both barrels.

The best-seller lay facedown on Emma's lap. She mentally practiced several versions of her speech. None of them sounded adequate. Emma checked her phone, then tapped it disgustedly against the chair's upholstered arm. She hadn't really expected to receive the DNA results from Genetix yesterday, despite their one-day-service advertising. But she'd received no calls today, either. She phoned the lab. A recording. Did people ever stay at their desks? Frowning, she left a message. Emma stared out the window of her nook, watching slow-moving cars weave in and out of the hospital entrance. She bought and drank a diet cola she didn't want. Finally the hour expired. She marched to Kevin's room.

He'd begun to stir, and when Emma entered, his eyes opened. The joy sparkling in them hit her like shrapnel. She wanted to dive for cover.

Kelly rose, patted Emma on the shoulder, and said, "I'm going for coffee."

Good. Her partner had positioned the chair farther away from Kevin's bed. Emma made herself smile as she sat. "Feeling better?"

"Now that you're here."

The words she'd rehearsed shriveled.

"I've even begun to think about when I leave this place. For a while I wasn't sure I would." A grin tugged at his mouth. "Dottie Faye would take credit for that, but you're the reason I made it." The magnetic silver eyes refused to release hers. "You're the reason I wanted to make it."

No, no, no. Emma swallowed. "Kevin, you have everything to live for. You're a brilliant actor with a bright future."

"But when I was offstage, I felt like a prisoner doing time." He shook his head. "No, when I'm with you, I do things I can't do alone. I can be more than I am." He raised his head, face shining like a child's.

"I was glad to be there for you when you were so sick, but ..."

"Not exactly a fun way to start a relationship." He grinned ruefully. "Now that I'm better, we can build it in a positive, more balanced way." He leaned from the bed so far that she scrambled to help him. He touched her face. "Emma, I know I fall short in a hundred ways, but I want to be there for you too. I want to make you as happy as you make me."

Much, much worse than I thought.

She edged away and said quietly, "Kevin, I'm sorry."

"Sorry? Because you haven't come to see me as much? Dottie Faye didn't make it easy." The smile that had captured a thousand women widened.

"No. I'm sorry because I haven't been honest with you. Kevin, I don't feel the same way you do."

The smile stayed in place, as if too stunned to move. But his eyes turned the color of storm clouds, no silver lining in sight. Silence for a full minute. Then, in a voice stretched like wire, he said, "Perhaps you might explain why, when I was dying, you held my hand and willed me back?"

"I did pray for you." She tried to choose her words carefully. "I was horrified at what had happened to you. But I didn't know you well. And ... I had an additional reason for hoping you survived."

"You wanted something." His smile sharpened into a weapon. "That shouldn't surprise me. Everyone does." A tremor disturbed the perfect plane of his voice. "But I thought you were different, Emma."

"I—I am." She cringed at the hurt huddled in that small quaver. "Please listen."

He lay back against the bed, arms crossed, and stared at nothing while she told him about Rose. When she paused for breath, he said incredulously, "But the police questioned me—and everyone else in that class—fifteen years ago. I was sorry to hear of her death, but didn't they conclude that she fell down the stairs?"

"It was a cover-up!" Emma cried. She explained the new evidence they had mysteriously received. She described the class quilt.

"Yeah, I made a block for that." Kevin fiddled with his bed controls.

"We're contacting every person from that class," Emma said. "That's why we came to New York. To find you." She took a deep breath. "Do you remember why you and Rose argued?"

"Argued?" He looked at Emma as if she were an alien.

"The day before she died," Emma probed.

Kevin's head rose from the bed like a cobra's. "You think I killed her?"

She looked at her hands.

"You've thought that all along." So frail for so long, Kevin now frightened her. His eyes, molten silver, burned with fury. "I believed you were a kind, caring woman."

You don't even know me—

"A woman I wanted to know and love. Instead," he spat the words out, "you were stalking me, trying to nail me for a murder I didn't commit."

"I wasn't stalking you, Kevin." Despite her trembling insides, Emma kept her voice firm. "Remember that we protected you, night and day, when the police wouldn't?"

"Because you cared, right?" His bitterness poisoned the air.

"Yes," Emma choked out. "We care about you, and we care about the truth. What about you, Kevin?"

He sneered, "Do you care enough about the truth to believe me? I only vaguely remember the woman. You're right, I probably argued with her. At that age, I argued with all my profs—but I'm sure it was trivial."

Kevin would never admit to anything. She saw it in his rigid face, in his fists clenching the bedsheets.

"No," he said. "I can see you'll never believe me." The liquid fire in his eyes cooled and hardened. Kevin sliced her with his words. "You're out of your mind if you think I'm a murderer."

Emma moved her mouth. No words came out.

"Leave. Before I do something I'll regret." He thundered, "Get out of here!"

She fled the room, shaking. For the first time, Kevin looked like a killer.

nineteen

"I am glad you told Kevin that you weren't meant to be together. It had to be done." Dottie Faye nibbled one of Lucinda's homemade cinnamon doughnuts as she, Emma, and Kelly shared a sumptuous breakfast with their hostess in her sunny three-season room. "But I wish you had let me know ahead of time so I could have prepared the poor boy." Her blue eyes glinted.

Translation: "You left me out of the loop again, sweet peas, and I won't soon forget it." Emma buttered her banana nut muffin so vigorously it crumbled. Kelly fidgeted in her wicker chair.

Her aunt fluttered reproachful eyelashes at Emma. "And I wish you had asked my advice, Emma Jane, before you spoke with him."

"He understood me." Emma was done discussing this subject.

"A lady doesn't just dump a gentleman like trash." Dottie's voice dwindled to a tone as delicate as her lacy satin robe. "You do it with sweetness, with flair, and gentle regret."

With difficulty, Emma kept her voice down. "I tried to be honest."

"Don't worry your head about it for a minute, honey. I'll help him recover." A cat-that-ate-the-canary smile contradicted Dottie Faye's virtuous words.

While Kelly and Lucinda gave Emma twin looks of sympathy, Emma struggled to hold her temper.

When Genetix had called back late yesterday, they informed

her they had never received Kevin's sample. The expensive courier service assured her they'd "check on it." And after yesterday's blowup with Kevin, Emma wanted only peace. Was that too much to ask? Why did Dottie continue to insert sugary barbs into their conversations?

"Jealousy, plain and simple," Kelly told her afterward when they'd retreated to Emma's room. "She hovered over Kevin till late last night. I can't imagine her consolation helped much. Not fun, knowing your crush misses somebody else."

Emma groaned and flopped full length onto the bed. Living with Dottie Faye had proved challenging in the past— her aunt moved in with Emma, uninvited, after her mother's death to "help." Dottie Faye had finally found a large colonial mansion in Mystic Harbor and had moved out of Emma's cottage. Now Emma couldn't face life in the same house with her aunt again for one more day. "I need space. I need time away from Dottie Faye. Now."

"Me too," Kelly sighed, "but I'm sorry I have to leave today." Her daughter Julie, who attended a college in upstate New York, had arranged an overnight shopping trip to introduce Kelly to her boyfriend's mother. "Where will you go tonight? I can't leave you alone."

"Don't be ridiculous. I'll tell Lucinda I'm going to a hotel, and I'll be just fine." Emma tried to smile. "Dottie Faye needs time away from me too."

Kelly wouldn't back down. "New York's a lonely place without a friend."

"You know this is important to Julie." Emma dug in both heels. Her friend shouldn't miss a special time with her daughter because of a tiff between Emma and Dottie Faye.

"Then I won't leave until you're settled in a new place." Kelly crossed her arms.

"We'd better tell Lucinda and Dottie Faye." *Before I back out.*

They found the two women in Lucinda's palatial all-white living room, sitting by the glowing marble fireplace.

"We've so enjoyed our time here," Emma clasped their kind hostess's hand, "but Kelly and I think we've imposed on your hospitality long enough." Emma explained their plans.

Lucinda vociferously objected, but Dottie said little. Emma hadn't realized that deep down, she'd hoped her aunt would protest loudly that no niece of hers was going to stay in some crummy second-rate hotel.

Emma pasted on a smile. "Thanks, but we think this is best."

After she and Kelly packed, they said goodbye in the front foyer. Lucinda's soft face pillowed a sad smile. "I wish I could keep you girls here forever."

Dottie gave Emma a polite hug. "Sweet pea, you take care, bless your little heart."

Emma suspected that Dottie used "Bless your little heart" as a code for "I hope you choke on your grits."

As Emma fought traffic en route to the hotel, she comforted herself that Dottie tended to erupt for no reason and then forgive for no reason. Hopefully, this storm would end before it turned into a hurricane.

A second-story, boxlike, musty hotel room with a view of two dumpsters didn't compare with Lucinda's house. Emma, toting luggage up the stairs, tried to look on the bright side. *With no elevator, I won't feel dizzy.*

"Be extra careful." Kelly tested the deadbolts on the door. "And no night stakeouts." She frowned. "I don't like your being in New York by yourself."

The prospect didn't leave Emma warm and fuzzy either, but she ignored her doubts. "I'll be fine."

"What will you do while I'm gone?"

Emma's fists clenched. "First, I plan to visit the manager of that courier company."

"I know it's important, but are you sure you should?" Kelly eyed her.

"I promise to behave." *Sort of.*

"Good." Kelly zipped her overnight bag. "We don't need any more murders."

At the subway station, they headed in different directions. By the time Emma stalked across the company's threshold, her simmering anger had reached the boiling point.

"We're doing all we can to find your package, Ms. Cotton." The plump, pink-faced manager wrung his hands. "We'll send it the minute we track it down."

"Not good enough," Emma growled.

"And we'll refund your money."

"That's only reasonable, given the service I've received. Update me tomorrow." She flung "There are some things more important than money!" at him as she stomped out the door.

Instead of taking the subway to touch base with Detective Baines, Emma walked until her fury cooled and she could think.

We'd better try to harvest another sample from Kevin as insurance.

But how? Kevin hated her now. Kelly was gone. And at this point, Emma certainly couldn't communicate with Dottie Faye.

Her frustration mounted when the police station desk officer told her Baines was on vacation for two weeks. She walked until she felt ready to drop.

Emma entered a ladies' room at a fast food restaurant and donned the wig Dottie had bought her and her Dottie Cam flower. She followed Madison from The Paddington, but the woman entered a coffeehouse alone. She appeared to study scripts. Emma sat in a booth at the far end of the room. Now drained, she thumbed through her fabric sample book, hoping it would stimulate her creative juices and keep her alert.

Even the new fabrics' beauty failed to invigorate her. Emma dozed off, then awoke to find Madison gone. The baristas aimed deep frowns in her direction. She decided to go back to the hotel before she was arrested for loitering or, worse, got mugged.

Emma returned to the hotel and crashed. She came to an hour later, feeling as if she'd awakened inside a black hole. She couldn't think well inside this vacuum.

Dottie had more than hinted that Kevin had suffered a relapse. Emma doubted her aunt's claim, but doubts nibbled, then gnawed on her. Emma pounded a pillow, and then she called his hospital floor.

"I'm sorry. I can't release information on Mr. Crawford." Compassion colored the nurse's words. She hesitated, then said, "He also instructed us to inform you that you are not permitted in his room."

Air whooshed out of Emma the way it did out of pounded pillows. "I see. Thank you."

If Kevin could issue dictums, he certainly wasn't near death. Emma fluffed her hair in the mirror. She grabbed her bag and umbrella because the sun had left town while she had napped. She headed through the cheerless streets to the nearest subway station.

Emma didn't know where she was going or what she was doing, but she'd develop a plan on the way.

Of course she would.

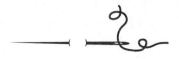

It was the last place on earth Emma expected to visit.

Well, not the last, but certainly in the bottom ten.

The Empire State Building loomed above her, a massive stone-and-glass giant full of elevators and dizzying views.

What am I doing here?

Kelly had dared Emma to put the building on their must-see list. She agreed if Kelly, who hated caves and other subterranean spaces, would drive with her through one of New York's tunnels. They'd managed to avoid both places.

Until now.

Emma entered the shining lobby and bought a ticket.

I stood in line to see the Constitution and the Declaration of Independence. To experience Disney World. But to ride an elevator?

She and the other lunatics crammed into the cubicle and rode, bunched like celery stalks, to the observation deck.

With rivulets of sweat dripping down her face, Emma hoped her deodorant was working. The effectiveness of the other passengers' antiperspirants didn't concern her, as Emma held her breath all eighty-six floors.

By the time they reached the top, Emma couldn't move. No problem. Her fellow riders, released from prison, carried her out onto the open-air deck.

The wicked wind yanked at her hair and coat. Emma didn't dare look up at the 102nd story and the post originally intended for dirigible parking. She wanted to hug a wall but forced herself toward the rail. *If you don't take at least one picture, Kelly will never believe this.*

Emma clung to the rail. Somber cloud ghosts haunted the building, with small hoary patches, like bearded gnomes, leering from below. The Hudson River had donned its most solemn garb, with monolithic barges seemingly frozen in time. Thousands upon thousands of buildings, whose pale lights only emphasized their starkness, emptied the scene of life. Quaking, Emma raised her phone and took a photo.

OK, so the shot looked blurry and less than inspiring. *It's proof I was here.*

Undaunted by the weather, numerous couples cuddled, kissed, and posed for pictures. Several proposals seemed imminent, à la *An Affair to Remember* and *Sleepless in Seattle.*

Emma didn't envy them. She truly harbored no interest in marrying, at least not now. But the cooing of pigeons and the couples grated on her. Her best friend had left. Emma knew only two other people in New York City well, and they preferred to ignore her. God seemed silent too.

Had that been the reason she'd come here? Perhaps she'd sought an urban Mount Sinai, a place to meet with Him?

Trembling, she clutched the rail as afternoon merged into early evening. The wind drove tiny needles of moisture into her cheeks. She stared at the sad gray city. Off to the west, clouds piled in huge purple mountains.

Emma's open jaw froze so rain-needles pierced her tongue. She didn't know how long she stood, watching the tempest build. Emma bowed her head to shield her face from sleet that the angry wind aimed like dozens of blades.

Tour guides yelled for everyone to head inside. The crowd wandered toward the elevator, some grabbing a final photo. Emma slowly unlocked cold fingers from the rail.

But before she turned to go, the city exploded in a glow that took away what was left of her breath. Thousands of golden streetlight halos chased the darkness away. Wave upon wave of neon-light rainbows filled the city, their shine only enhanced by the storm. Christmas lights twinkled on a thousand homes and businesses, promising even greater joy.

At home in Mystic Harbor, sunrises over the Atlantic reminded Emma of God's presence and power.

Though she hadn't believed it, He also lived in New York City.

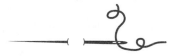

"Lucinda has invited you to tea with us tomorrow at four." Though courteous, Dottie's voice on the phone held all the warmth of an airport announcement. But Emma wouldn't have considered saying no. She showed up on Lucinda's doorstep, where she was greeted by her enthusiastic hostess and a less eager Dottie. Emma encouraged herself that her aunt had progressed in her attitude. At least she didn't bless Emma's heart.

She had genuinely missed Lucinda, who served as a buffer. But a phone call from one of her charities sent Lucinda out the door soon after they began eating.

Emma helped herself to more delectable scones and ripe strawberries with cream. She'd forgotten to eat lunch, and these would make up for the unidentifiable pastries she'd encountered at her hotel's free breakfast bar.

Dottie set down her teacup. "Emma Jane, we will not waste time discussing your disastrous session with Kevin."

OK. Emma chewed her scone more than necessary. *Then what's on the agenda?*

"First, I want you to understand," Dottie Faye said, fixing Emma with a severe blue gaze, "that I would never, ever go through anyone's personal belongings except when my conscience demands it."

At her righteous expression, laughter bubbled through cracks in Emma's rocklike resentment.

Dottie continued, "When I had dinner at Reed's a couple

of times, I borrowed his computer. I told him I needed to check my email. I did. But I saw some of his too."

"And?" Emma leaned forward, scones forgotten.

"I found emails from nasty people, bookies talking about Reed's bets. They said he owed thousands and thousands of dollars." Dottie clasped her hands. "Such language! I thought they were spam until I saw that Reed sent replies that were almost as bad!"

You go, Dottie Faye! Emma didn't know how this piece fit into their puzzle, but she wanted to hear more. "So Reed has a gambling problem?"

"Definitely. Such a shame. He can be quite the gentle-man—though he's a Yankee." Dottie sadly clicked her tongue. Then a conspiratorial smile blossomed on her face. "I don't take pictures with my phone. That's what cameras are for. But I tried, when Reed was busy doing something else. Most of the time, though, I ran my Dottie Cam while I sat at his desk."

Emma clapped. Dottie's smile widened. "But that's not all."

"It's not?"

"I found emails about Kevin from a Dr. Benton Giles. I checked with Kevin, and he's never heard of him. Kevin does keep track of these things."

Emma didn't doubt it. "What did Reed discuss with Dr. Giles?"

"Stuff about Kevin's medications and when he usually sleeps. He mentioned Brett's name once, though he didn't go into detail. He even mentioned me and the hours I'm at the hospital. Can you believe that?" Dottie preened, but declared, "It made no sense. I checked Reed's medicine cabinet when I used his bathroom. I read Dr. Giles's name on two of his medicine bottles, so he's Reed's doctor."

Emma mulled over her words. "Reed might ask Dr. Giles's

opinion about Kevin's treatments. But why mention Brett? And why would the doctor want to know about you?"

"I have no idea. There's even more." Dottie Faye leaned forward, her eyes glittering. "I haven't gone out with Reed as much lately; I was afraid he had begun to catch on to me. But I'm glad I went yesterday. I pretended to forget my phone and borrowed his. He's been texting Dr. Giles all the time about Kevin and me. He talks to those bookies too—though they call him much more than he calls them."

Emma's pulse quickened. "I wonder if Giles is the same doctor who treated Brett at The Paddington." If only Kelly were here, with her smartphone and her techie touch! "May I use your laptop?"

"Sure." In her enjoyment of this one-sided revelation, Dottie Faye had forgotten to remain distant. "But don't mess with it too much, Emma Jane. With Kelly Ann away, who will fix it if its hormones act up?"

Dottie Faye brought the laptop to the table, and Emma searched for Dr. Giles's picture. "Here he is. He's an internist. He has a practice and is on staff with several hospitals."

"Let me look at him too." Dottie Faye hunched over Emma. They squinted at the picture of the balding fifty-something man. Dottie Faye shook her head. "That's not the doctor who went backstage with Brett. He had a beard."

"Even if Dr. Giles had a beard, I don't think it's the same man." Emma wilted. "Brett's doctor was younger and heavier, with darker eyes and hair."

Dottie nodded, her forehead creasing until she remembered to smooth it out. "My my. I don't know what to make of all this."

"I don't either." Emma dared pat her aunt on the shoulder. "But you've done excellent detective work, Aunt Dottie, and I have a feeling all these clues fit together somehow."

"Don't call me that, Emma Jane." Nevertheless, Dottie looked pleased.

Hearing her aunt chime in with her usual rebuke warmed Emma's heart. "I'm sorry, Dottie Faye."

"All this talk about Kevin worries me, though. The latest texts on Reed's phone seemed to hint something big was going to happen soon." Dottie twisted and turned her giant solitaire diamond ring. "I'll stick closer than ever to Kevin, especially since the policeman won't be there as much."

Emma looked up sharply. "When did that happen?"

"Yesterday." Dottie frowned. "When the policeman didn't show by noon, I called the station. They said something about being low on manpower because of an unusual number of family emergencies. They need to keep overtime to a minimum because they'll have to call up every available officer for the holidays."

"Then no one's guarding Kevin?" Emma blurted.

"He has me." Dottie crossed her arms.

At the gleam in her eye, a chill rippled down Emma's spine. In the past, Dottie Faye had used firearms when she felt conditions warranted them.

"Don't worry, Emma Jane." Her aunt seemed to read Emma's mind. "I would never take a gun to a hospital. It just wouldn't be proper."

"Or legal." Emma exhaled.

"Plus, the station did say they'd try to send an officer at night."

"At least you won't have to do night duty." No doubt, Kevin would appreciate a break from her ever-present aunt. Emma said carefully, "I wish I could help, but since that's not possible, I'm glad Kevin has a good friend like you."

"I stand by my friends." Dottie lifted her chin. "And I

stand by my kin, even if she doesn't know diddly-squat about letting a man down gracefully."

Ignoring her rising irritation, Emma let her hug say it all. She thought about mentioning the need for a second DNA sample, but why complicate her tenuous truce with Dottie Faye? Kelly would return late tonight. She could try to collect the sample tomorrow.

"I see things are looking up?" Lucinda reentered the room and patted Emma on the shoulder.

Dottie announced, "Emma Jane would like to come back and stay awhile, if that's all right with you."

Excuse me? Emma's annoyance caught in her throat like a dry, oversized pill, but she swallowed it anyway.

"I'd love that!" Lucinda clapped her hands. "It seems like forever since you left. We've missed you girls."

No more silence. No more black hole. Emma said, "That would be wonderful."

"Let's celebrate by going out to eat tonight at Le Bernardin. I'll make reservations." Lucinda pulled out her phone.

Emma blinked. "Will they take them this late?"

Her hostess pshawed. "I'll talk them into it."

Emma believed her. Lucinda—along with her money— possessed a gift for accomplishing little miracles. Had her understated nudge helped initiate this meeting?

Dottie Faye stood. "Please make the reservations for two, not three, Lucinda. I'll be at the hospital the rest of the evening." She checked her watch. "In fact, I should leave in twenty minutes if I want to make the next subway."

Emma pecked her on the cheek. "I know you'll keep Kevin safe."

Frothing at the mouth, but safe.

twenty

"It's so good to have you back. I wish I could go in with you."
Emma turned to Kelly as they sat in Emma's Jeep outside
Benton Giles's posh medical office. Both she and Kelly feared
he or his staff would recognize Emma from newspaper photos.

"What's to worry about? I'm a nice, middle-aged lady
tourist, with a husband and kids, who has migraines and likes
to talk. One of millions." Kelly opened her door. "I'm just glad
Lucinda's best friend is one of Giles's patients."

"Otherwise, you'd never get an appointment this quickly."
Emma resolved to make their hostess and friend a special thank-
you gift. Her throat tightened as she watched her friend cross
the parking lot to the office entrance. *Waiting again.* She'd
learned to dislike doctors' offices before her mother died, but
killing time while Kelly gently probed the psyche of a possible
psychopath chilled Emma.

Stop fussing. Kelly will handle him.

Emma shifted to the passenger's side and opened her laptop,
forcing herself to concentrate on files Kelly had created from
Dottie Cam videos.

What a shame her aunt's picture-taking attempts on her
phone hadn't worked. The flower camera had bobbed up and
down with Dottie's every movement, blurring the cramped
font of the emails. Emma caught a word here, a line there,
but not sufficient evidence to corroborate Dottie's assertions.

Only enough to possibly indict her aunt for sneaking
around Reed's computer.

Emma gulped. She finished the videos, and to her amazement, the courier service manager called. "We found your package and sent it out immediately!" He launched into volumes of regrets without explanations. Emma wanted to explode again. But she clipped his tirade with a stiff acceptance of his apology and hung up.

Kelly appeared a few minutes later. Emma told her about the courier. "That DNA had better reach the lab this time. We should hear from them on Monday." She said, "I'd feel better if we harvested a second sample, just in case. Do you think you could do it?"

"And send it with a different courier?" Kelly grimaced. "I'll try today, because Kevin's doctor talked about dismissing him early next week."

"Time's running out on us." Now Emma felt a migraine coming on. She ignored it. "How did your session with Dr. Giles go?"

"He said my headaches will vanish if I return to Mystic Harbor and take a long rest." Kelly smiled wryly. "The man didn't bat an eye when I mentioned Kevin and his play, but his nurse flinched."

"Maybe she hates Shakespeare." Emma pulled out of the parking lot. "So Dr. Giles wants you to go home, huh? Perhaps he wants to get rid of you?"

"Probably." Kelly wrinkled her nose. "The doctor is friendly to a fault and polite to the point I don't trust him." She cracked her window. "Let's go to Central Park. I need a walk and fresh air."

Emma gladly complied. Unseasonably warm weather reigned, though that soon would change. Kelly knelt and swashed a hand in the Burnett Fountain. Exotic goldfish darted away. "So … from Dottie's snooping, the nurse's reaction, and his, we might suspect the good doctor and Reed both were involved in Kevin's poisoning."

"I think so." Emma dropped beside her. "Yet, why would Dr. Giles take a risk like that? I checked his credentials. No black spots on his record. He's been practicing for decades, and he's in good standing at the hospitals. I even found newspaper articles about his community service."

"And we hit a wall with Reed as a suspect. He had excellent financial incentives to keep both Kevin and Brett alive." Kelly scratched her head.

"Madison had a much clearer motive to kill Kevin. But if she did it, how is she connected with Reed and Giles?" Emma fretted. "As usual, we're uncovering more questions than answers. At least we can commiserate."

"We're always better together. But I'm glad I spent time with Julie and her maybe future mother-in-law. We needed to start off on the right foot." Kelly checked her phone and chuckled. "Herbie just texted me. He's asking if we can talk Dottie out of spending every waking moment with Kevin. She's driving him crazy."

"I doubt it. Dottie probably stands guard outside his bathroom door." Emma smiled too, then sobered. "Reed and Giles's emails hinted of an upcoming 'event.' She's convinced something big will happen soon, and I tend to agree with her."

"She's still sweet on him, right?"

"Oh yes. I think part of this fixation involves motherly instinct. She doesn't associate him with Rose's murder anymore. He's her boy, and she'll fight aliens to protect him." Emma shook her head. "She still believes Kevin's her ticket to stardom. And she loves the attention. Reporters chase her now like they did me." Emma didn't mind that turnaround.

Kelly swished the water again. "Herbie and I try to give Kevin a break." The teen had spent much of his free time visiting his friend.

"Talk about irony." Emma clasped her hands behind her head. "He may have been protecting him from his own dad!"

Kelly groaned. "Nothing about this case is simple."

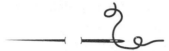

The next morning complicated it even more. Kelly's call from the hospital caught Emma lying in bed, trying to talk herself into getting up.

Her partner sounded half-amused, half-irritated. "Did Dottie Faye mention having plans last night? Kevin said that after a few hours, she left him without warning. He was relieved at first, but then wondered if he'd upset her."

"When people tick Dottie Faye off, she makes it *very* clear." Emma frowned. "It's not like her to walk out without telling someone. I'll sound her out when I hear her stir."

While Emma dressed, she kept an ear trained on Dottie's room. Nothing. Emma wandered down to the kitchen for coffee and greeted Lucinda, who carried her flight bag.

Emma had forgotten about her hostess's meeting in Chicago. "Have a great trip." Emma hugged her. "By the way, have you talked to Dottie Faye this morning?"

"Not a word. She and I usually wind different clocks, you know." Lucinda winked and departed. Emma knew better than to disturb Dottie's beauty sleep, but by ten o'clock, worry about her blood pressure medicine sent Emma tapping on her door. "Aunt Dottie?"

She listened for the familiar rebuke.

Silence.

Maybe her aunt was enjoying the spa? Emma poked her head in.

The bathroom door was open.

And no one had slept in the bed.

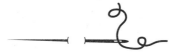

"You say your aunt's sixty-six years old. Is she in her right mind?" the officer quizzed Emma.

"Yes." She sometimes wondered about Dottie's sanity, but she would never disappear like this.

"Sorry." He shrugged. "If she chooses to spend the night with her boyfriend, we can't do much about it. If she's still missing after twenty-four hours, call us."

You guys sound like Tom Boyer. Emma bit her lip. "Thanks."

Emma strode out of the station, her thoughts caught in a seething whirlpool. She had called Herbie, who gave her Reed's number. Voice mail. Voice mail. Voice mail. Emma wanted to scream.

Instead, she called Kelly at the hospital. "I'm getting nowhere. Can you talk Kevin into letting me see him?"

"I'll try." Emma heard brief murmurs, then Kelly again. "He says he will."

"Good," Emma said as she passed through the hospital entrance, "because I'll be there in five minutes."

Perhaps they were overreacting. Emma decided not to call Lucinda quite yet. Perhaps her aunt had wandered onto somebody else's stage. Maybe she'd opened the Dottie Faye Detective School, with required uniforms: big-hair wigs and Dottie Cam flowers.

Half-laughing, half-crying, Emma entered Kevin's room. She knew she looked a mess. Kevin, on the other hand, wore a calm expression as he told her what she already knew: Dottie

Faye had hovered around him for four hours last night, then excused herself around nine thirty "for a few minutes" and never returned.

"Do you think Dottie's found a new venture?" Kevin addressed the wall behind her and Kelly, reminding Emma of how she had talked to his nose when they first met.

"Dottie Faye might be juggling four or five crazy new projects, and we wouldn't know," Kelly said. "But she'd never walk out on a friend—not without an explanation."

Emma locked onto Kelly's words. Of course, her partner was right. Though Emma hadn't learned anything new from Kevin, he hadn't negated what they believed to be true. She appreciated his breaking the vow of silence.

"Thanks for seeing me." Emma poured gratitude into her gaze.

He didn't smile, but his stiff mouth relaxed slightly. "It was the least I could do. If I can help in any other way ..."

"We might take you up on that," Kelly spoke up. "Emma has an idea. I can tell."

Emma nodded. "Since the police won't investigate yet, I'd like to examine the hospital's security videos from last night."

"You think the guards will just hand those over?" Kevin's lip curled. "And what does this have to do with me?"

"With your help, I think I can talk them into it."

Emma explained her plan, and Kevin agreed. "If it works, fine. I'll do it."

She flinched through the elevator ride to the basement, where the security office was located. A guard she didn't know lounged behind the desk, watching feeds from security cameras.

Spotting his name tag, Emma greeted him with her most winning smile. "Mr. Court, can you tell me when Dan Greeson is on duty?" Dan, Kevin's fervent fan, had checked on him more frequently than required.

"He comes in at three." Matthew Court shifted his feet to the floor. "Maybe I can help you?"

Emma didn't think so, but every minute counted right now. "Have you heard of Kevin Crawford?"

"Actually, I'm glad I wasn't assigned to him," Court said with a scowl. "I spent a bundle on tickets for his show. My girlfriend thinks he's wonderful." He snorted. "Well, Mr. Wonderful overdosed, didn't he? The theater gave me a refund, but Tiffany's been a pain ever since."

Not a promising situation, but Emma upped the charm another notch. "Do you think his autograph would smooth things over with her?"

"Maybe." The man's face brightened. "But the bosses told everyone to leave him alone. Period."

"Kevin will give you his autograph if I ask him," Emma said coyly.

Court narrowed his eyes. "I see. And you will do that if …?"

"If you allow me to review some recent security videos."

A kaleidoscope of gladness, suspicion, and frustration flickered over his face. "Nothing's happened that's worth watching," the guard growled. "Who are you, anyway?"

Desperation swelled in her throat. "I'm Emma Cotton. My elderly aunt and I are close friends of Kevin's. She visited him yesterday and then wandered off, and no one's seen her since. I'm almost out of my mind with worry, but the police won't look for her for twenty-four hours."

The anger in Court's face faded. "Look, lady, I'd love to help you—"

"I'll arrange for you and your girlfriend to visit Kevin for twenty minutes. Today."

Eyes wide, he glanced at his watch. "I can get someone to cover for me. Tiffany's off work today." Court's face hardened.

"I can't disappoint her again. How do I know this will happen?"

How do I know you'll help me? Nevertheless, Emma pointed to his computer. "Kevin's in room 407. You can check that yourself. I'll call him on the hospital phone. You can say a few words as well. Will that suffice?"

Her ploy won him over. After they spoke with Kevin, the guy called his girlfriend.

"She'll be here soon." A giant grin spread across his face. "This will make Tiffany's year."

Court set Emma up in a back room with a computer. "Yesterday's videos, all three shifts. If you need more, let me know." He lowered his voice. "You'll keep quiet about our little deal?"

"Not a word." Emma closed an imaginary zipper across her mouth. "I just want to find my aunt."

She pulled up the evening-shift fourth-floor video first and ran its time to nine o'clock. The camera, apparently located near the elevator, scanned the long corridor, including the nurses' station, and the shorter horizontal hall that intersected near it. The blurry black-and-white video wouldn't win prizes, but Emma could make out faces fairly well. Most visitors had come and gone. The elevator opened several times for a few doctors and nurses, some of whom Emma recognized. Techs and aides pushed machines and gurneys past the camera. Emma kept one eye on Kevin's room. The lights in the hallway dimmed, as they always did that time of evening. Emma squinted at the stairwell door at the far end of the long hall. No sign of movement.

She inhaled when Dottie Faye exited Kevin's room. Whatever she said to the nurses at the station made two grin, while another rolled her eyes. Emma's aunt, wearing an enormous Dottie Cam flower, strode toward the elevator, looking so vital, so smiley, so Dottie Faye that Emma reached toward the monitor. Her aunt opened a compact and preened as the elevator doors closed, and she disappeared from sight.

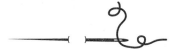

"Any sign of your aunt in the ER entrance video?" Court, who had morphed to "Matthew" since his girlfriend's dream visit with Kevin, peered over Emma's shoulder.

"Not yet." After several hours, Emma's eyeballs felt like rocks, yet she couldn't shift her gaze from the monitor. She ran the ER video again.

Strangers with desperate faces entered, clutching crying children or white-faced, gasping elderly men or women. Two flashing ambulances pulled up, EMTs shouting information to medical staff as they plunged patients on gurneys through automatic doors, frantic family in their wake.

No Dottie Faye.

Emma held her head in her hands, then straightened. *You have no time to fall apart.* She forced her eyes back to the monitor.

The aroma of steaming coffee wafted past her nose. Matthew placed a paper cup beside her. "You look like you could use a pick-me-up."

"Thanks." She sipped it. A flicker on the screen grabbed her eye. Why? Emma paused the video, then ran it back. There it was again—a man's profile, barely within the camera's range, speaking briefly to a nurse. Emma leaned forward. She didn't know him—or did she?

Giles. Dr. Benton Giles. He was on staff at Metro Memorial. "Matthew, do the doctors have a separate hospital entrance?"

He nodded. "One to the north that leads to the employee

parking garage, and one door on the south side, near their private lot." He looked at her curiously. "Why?"

Emma kept her tone even. "I thought Dottie Faye might have wandered to the wrong area by mistake."

"That's possible, though I'd think a doc would have reported her."

"You don't know my aunt. She may be a little crazy, but she can outwit anyone." Emma forced a smile. "May I see those entrance videos too?"

"Sure." He brought up several files.

"I'm glad you're back in Tiffany's good graces," Emma said as she hurriedly opened the files. She fast-forwarded the north garage entrance video and squinted at a number of doctors who entered and exited. Some looked vaguely familiar.

The south entrance appeared almost deserted. Emma remembered the storm that had awakened her that night. No one wanted to park outside on a night like that. Her eyes nearly popped out of her head when a tall figure, looking anxiously over his shoulder, appeared on the monitor.

Reed!

He opened the door a slit and seemed to look around. Apparently satisfied, he turned and gestured toward the camera. The back of another tall man appeared, a bald man pushing someone in a wheelchair.

Turn and look toward me! Emma begged.

He didn't. Frantically she scanned files and found one that taped the entire parking lot. She whipped through it and, at the sight of the two men, slowed it.

Darkness kept Emma from seeing clearly, but together, they loaded someone into a taxi.

Someone who wasn't moving.

twenty-one

When *we return to Mystic Harbor, I'll have to learn to drive all over again.* As they screeched around yet another corner, Emma glanced at Kelly, who had just finished phoning Lucinda, then Kevin. "Everybody OK?" Emma asked.

"Return flights from Chicago have been grounded because of high winds, so Lucinda's taking the train. She sounds totally panicked." Kelly sighed. "And I wish Herbie hadn't visited Kevin today. He's completely clueless that his dad is involved in this mess. What if Reed tries to pull something while we're gone?"

"I know." Emma's stomach lurched even more than her Jeep. "But maybe Reed will hold off if Herbie's there. *Someone* needs to stick with Kevin. And I need your help, Kelly. We don't know what this day will bring."

Kelly rechecked the Mace and small tool kits they would carry. "When Herbie took a bathroom break, Kevin told the nurses to call security if Reed sets a toe on the floor. I told Herbie to call us if Dr. Giles—or any other doctor Kevin doesn't know—comes near the room."

"Good. Now help me find this taxi place."

Kelly and her phone guided them to the Manhattan Move-It Taxi Company, a dingy building squeezed between other dingy buildings. Though Emma begged the owner to tell her the address where her elderly aunt had been transported the night before, he fixed her with a cold stare. "I don't give out addresses. If Auntie wanted you to know where she was goin', she'd have told you."

"But these men took her against her will," Emma pleaded. "She was unconscious."

"So call the cops." He shrugged and walked back toward his garage.

Emma's fists clenched. How she ached to beat the information out of him!

Kelly touched Emma's elbow, a reminder that doing jail time for assault would not help Dottie. Emma watched his disappearing back, her hope vanishing with him.

"Excuse me," someone whispered behind them. "Maybe I can help."

Emma turned to see a fiftyish woman with a weary, lined face. She half-sat on the hood of a taxi, parked just beyond the front windows of the garage. Emma and Kelly slowly walked toward the woman, avoiding eye contact in case her boss was watching.

The driver leafed through a newspaper. "Your aunt was taken somewhere in one of our taxis?"

Emma pretended to talk to Kelly. "Yes. They took her from Metro Memorial Hospital last night around nine thirty."

"Did you see the taxi ID number?"

"Seven B twenty-three."

"I'll nose around. See you at the doughnut shop across the street in half an hour."

Emma and Kelly looked at each other.

"Why would she help us?" Kelly's eyebrows reached her hairline.

"I have no idea. But if angels moonlight as cab drivers, she's definitely one of them." Emma gestured across the street. "Do you think you could force yourself to eat doughnuts?"

"I'm always ready to do my duty."

Though the shop's ambiance left a bit to be desired, the

caramel cream-filled doughnuts sent Kelly into ecstasy. Emma's maple cruller lifted her spirits, though she wondered if their "angel" would follow through.

The cab driver did show. She ordered "the usual," then took her refreshments to a table near them. She returned to the coffee bar for a stirrer, dropping a paper napkin onto their table as she passed.

Emma blinked. Why the James Bond secrecy? Nevertheless, she read the penciled address on West 59th Street. Emma frowned. Had she seen it before?

Under the address, she saw a note: *My ex-daughter-in-law stole my grandson from the babysitter while I was at work.*

Tears welled in Emma's eyes. She turned to mouth "thank you" to the woman, but froze as she saw the taxi boss enter.

Well, that explains the cloak-and-dagger approach. She expressed her gratitude on another napkin and slipped it onto the woman's table as she went to the counter for a coffee refill.

Handing the counter clerk a hundred dollars, Emma said in a low voice, "I want to surprise that lady cab driver at the table by the window."

"You mean Ruthie?" The big man's dark face broke into a gleaming smile, but he kept his voice down as he refilled Emma's coffee. "She could use a nice surprise. Been missing her grandbaby something awful."

"Ruthie's coffee breaks are on me for awhile." Emma quickly returned to their table. They aimed quick glances of appreciation at Ruthie as they left. A tiny smile lit the woman's face.

Kelly, jogging alongside Emma's stride, fiddled with her phone's GPS. "Guess where we're going."

Emma set her jaw. "To visit the good doctor, right?"

They jumped into the Jeep. Emma peeled out of the parking

space. After another hair-raising ride, they pulled in by the black wrought-iron sign that bore the name of Benton H. Giles, M.D.

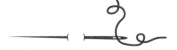

"Dr. Giles has left for the day." The receptionist answered Kelly's inquiry with a pleasant but firm tone.

"May I speak with his nurse? He told me it was important that I check in regularly."

A smiling dark-haired woman soon appeared behind the glass window, but she blinked when she saw Kelly.

The nurse tapped on the computer and pushed back the glass window. "Your records don't indicate that Dr. Giles required a return visit."

"He must have forgotten to type it in." Kelly twisted the hem of her top. "Please, may I come in and tell you how I'm feeling? I really think the doctor should know."

The nurse opened the door, though reluctantly, and Emma trailed Kelly, who continued to twist her top as she followed the nurse into an examining room.

After the woman closed the door, Kelly halted the nurse mid-turn with a rapier thrust: "We know Dr. Giles helped abduct Dottie Faye Sinclair and brought her here last night. Where is she?"

Fear glimmered in the woman's dark eyes, but she lifted her chin. "That is ridiculous. I have no idea what you're talking about."

"We think you do." Emma crossed her arms. "Dottie Faye is my aunt; a security video recorded Dr. Giles sneaking her out a hospital entrance last night. He brought her here. Did he take her someplace else?"

"Get out of here." Despite her tough words, terror sliced through the nurse's face.

"Certainly. We'll go to the police station." Kelly gestured to Emma, who plunged in her own rapier line: "You could be charged as an accessory, not only to kidnapping, but to murder. Does the name Brett Damon mean anything to you?"

The nurse blanched.

"Not to mention the attempted murder of Kevin Crawford."

"But Ben had nothing to do with those!" the nurse cried.

"Only kidnapping Aunt Dottie? So Dr. Giles retains his sainthood." Emma stood nose-to-nose with the nurse. "Sorry, lady, but your precious Ben is going down. If you don't tell me where my aunt is, you'll go down with him."

"He didn't want to do it," she sobbed. Her eyes flashed. "That awful man Reed Macklin talked him into it. If Ben weren't in terrible trouble—"

"He's in bigger trouble now, and he dragged you in with him." Kelly's voice softened. "He's not worth it. Tell us where Dottie Faye is, and we'll do our best not to implicate you when the police talk to us."

The nurse's head drooped. In a barely audible voice, she said, "He and Macklin took her to Maplehurst Senior Community."

"Where's that?" Kelly already was tapping on her phone.

"Upper West Side." The nurse covered her eyes and turned away.

"Thanks." Emma hurried out the door, her mind's gears racing faster than her heart.

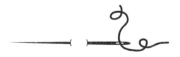

Maplehurst's head nurse stared at Emma, her voice icy. "That is outrageous. Dr. Giles has cared for patients here for years. We have the utmost respect for him."

"Nevertheless, it's true." Emma did not flinch. "If you'll take me to my aunt, she'll confirm every word."

"I told you before, I can't even tell you whether Dottie Sinclair is here. I haven't received a signed release." The woman's voice rose. "We cannot divulge medical information to every stranger who wanders our halls—without checking in at the front desk, I might add." She glared at Emma and Kelly.

"Then we'll remain here until Aunt Dottie signs a release." Emma sat on a cushy sofa while cockatiels, zebra finches, and lovebirds chirped in a nearby aviary. Kelly sat beside her.

"I'm calling the police," the head nurse declared.

"Good." Emma crossed her arms. "I was hoping to spare Maplehurst the publicity, but by all means, call them. They'll investigate and find we're telling the truth."

The nurse looked as if she wanted to throw the phone at Emma. Instead, she said, "I'll page Dr. Giles." Scowling, she spoke into an intercom.

Two tall men soon approached the nurses' station. Giles simply looked annoyed, but Reed's eyes bulged—for a second. Then he mirrored his partner's expression.

"Is there a problem, Sandra?" The doctor spoke in a courteous tone. "I thought we had discussed everything we needed to cover today."

"I'm sorry to bother you, doctor." She threw a frozen glance at Emma and Kelly. "These women are making the most bizarre claims. They said you brought their relative here against her will."

An incredulous smile touched his lips. "How ... interesting."

Emma wished she could squirt a water gun in his face—

anything to disrupt that almost noble expression he wore. "My aunt, Dottie Sinclair, would never have entered a facility like this. She's healthy and very, *very* capable of managing her own life."

"That's a total departure from reality, and you know it," Reed shot back. "You kept my sister from the care she needed because you want her money. But I'm not in Seattle anymore. Dr. Giles and I intend to restore her to health."

What?

Emma's lips turned to lead.

Kelly's didn't. "You lying, thieving creeps!" She shook her fist. "I can't believe you think you'll get away with this."

"Please have the decency to keep your voice down." Dr. Giles spoke in granite tones. "You'll frighten the patients."

A small shudder in Emma now swelled to a raging earthquake. "Is this how you carry out the Hippocratic Oath, doctor? Or in your case, the Hypocritical Oath?"

Pain flashed across his face, then vanished. "Sandra, would you call Ms. Lennox? Perhaps she can help us here."

The nurse already was on the phone, and a large, motherly looking woman appeared. "I'm Marilyn Lennox, the facility administrator. May I help you?"

"I have no idea. Will you?" Emma had moved past polite.

"I understand you are requesting information about a patient who may have been admitted here." She shook her head with a "there-there" smile. "I'm sorry, but we cannot release that without proper authorization. And if you disagree with Dr. Giles regarding your relative's treatment, surely that can be worked out."

"Dr. Giles and Reed Macklin, who, by the way, is *not* Dottie Faye Sinclair's brother"—Emma glowered at him—"have conspired to bring my aunt here without her consent. They claim we are gold-digging parasites." She shook with fury. "*They* are the parasites. I'm sure they plan to bilk her out of every penny she has."

"My, my." Ms. Lennox recoiled. "That's a very serious charge against a medical provider who is widely respected in Manhattan and in this facility. If you feel your complaint is valid, I suggest you take it up with the local medical association. But for now, I must ask you to leave before your behavior disrupts our entire community."

A burly, uniformed man appeared out of nowhere and fixed grim blue eyes on Emma and Kelly. He wore no gun, but he looked as if he could toss them into New Jersey.

Emma's heart sank lower than her stomach. Kelly pressed her shoulder lightly, signaling a retreat. Emma marched past Giles, who still looked properly outraged, and Reed, who threw them a gloating look as they stalked away.

Just wait, she railed at them silently. *If you think we've caved, you are in for one big surprise.*

twenty-two

"They're going to move Dottie," Kelly whispered as they exited Maplehurst's front door.

"Or they might just disappear—forever." Emma winced.

"No way! But we have to look as if we're leaving."

They said nothing more until they neared the parking lot.

"The nurses believe every word their precious Dr. Giles says. I'm sure the police will too—especially with Baines gone," Emma said with a scowl. "We're on our own for now. We'll call in the police when we have some proof."

Kelly nodded. "I can drop you off close to Maplehurst, then find a different parking lot."

"I'll sneak back and look for Dottie Faye." Emma's stride now matched her pulse. "I wish we'd had time to explore Maplehurst more thoroughly. I saw two wings in the building, A and B. I'll take A."

"I'll take B after I park." Kelly jogged beside her. "Let's text so we'll know how the other is doing."

They leaped into the Jeep. Kelly sped a few blocks away, then turned back toward Maplehurst and pulled over. Emma felt in her coat's large pocket for her Mace and the small plastic case of her toolbox, then hugged Kelly before throwing open her door.

"Be careful, Emma."

They clung for a moment before Emma rocketed from the car.

"Slow down, girl. You need to act like everything's normal." Kelly smiled and roared off.

Yeah, normal. Emma forced herself to stroll, her mind reviewing entrances she'd noticed at Maplehurst—probably locked with key codes at all times. Nursezilla and her staff surely prowled all three floors. Perhaps a service entrance might work? After all, someone had to empty the trash. She texted Kelly with the idea.

Maplehurst loomed before her. For the first time, Emma noticed the tall maple trees, shrubbery, and modern artwork that gave the facility its ambiance. Two odd-looking sculptures between the building and a tall fence graced a landscaped strip shaded by lengthening shadows. This time of year, only tufts of scraggly foliage clung to trees and bushes. Even so, they and the statues would help provide cover while she perused first-floor windows.

Shivering in the chilly wind, Emma circled to the back of the facility, then slunk behind an evergreen near an A wing window. She saw an aide handing a tiny, feeble-looking woman a water glass and medicine. Emma slipped from bush to sculpture to bush, probing each room's window, angling her gaze to inspect every bed and chair.

Where are you, Dottie Faye?

When she reached the building's end, Emma doubled back in case she'd missed a flash of Dottie's face or beehive—any indication her aunt was still alive.

At one window, an aide stared straight at Emma. She shrank against another evergreen, forbidding oxygen to enter her lungs. The man, apparently lost in his own thoughts, turned and left, leaving her gasping softly for breath and for hope—and thankful she'd worn her dark coat and knit hat yanked down over her hair.

Peering through the shadows, she examined the maples again. Two had sturdy, low-hanging branches that might enable her to climb for a second-floor view. Would the coming twilight provide sufficient cover?

Emma studied the silhouettes of the metal sculptures. One looked like a large, dark triangle of Swiss cheese. Not tall enough. The other, halfway between the trees with accessible branches, resembled a robot whose multiple arms might conceal her movements better than the trees. But the sculpture was located too far from the windows. Perhaps she could scale the robot first, then grab onto the taller tree's branches?

Kelly texted her. She'd followed a similar first-floor strategy. "Nothing so far. See you in ten at the service entrance?"

"Maybe," Emma replied. "Climbing trees to second floor first." She slipped from the shrub to the cheese sculpture. Emma knelt behind it, quickly shined her flashlight on her kit, and removed a glass cutter, a small hammer, and duct tape. She flicked off the light and returned them all to her coat pocket.

Emma's fingers slowly felt her way up the cold, rough metal structure and she climbed, thankful for her regular yoga sessions. She peered into the nearest second-story window. A short, bald man occupied one room. She craned her neck. A blond beehive in the next room! But it belonged to an aide. She couldn't see into the room on the other side of the little bald guy's. Emma edged toward one tree's low branch and slowly reached. When she grasped it and shifted her weight toward it, the limb creaked.

Blast. Emma curbed her impatience and traced a climbing path to the other side of the sculpture. The other tree's branch seemed sturdier. In the nearest room, an elderly man in a recliner watched a New York Knicks ball game with the volume so loud, Emma could hear the play-by-play. The next room was empty.

Yay! She grasped this branch, straddled it, and slid along it, the branch almost brushing the vacant room's window.

Her long arms that made sweater shopping a pain came in handy. She tried the window. Locked, of course.

Emma paused. Most quilters she knew couldn't be charged with breaking and entering. But their aunts hadn't been kidnapped either. Pulling out cutter and duct tape, Emma utilized a technique she'd learned while removing broken glass from storm windows. She etched several crisscrossing lines on a small area of the window near the lock, then stuck short strips of duct tape over them to keep shattered pieces from falling to the floor or ground. Pulling a mitten from her other pocket, she placed it against the window to muffle the hammer's tapping, though the raucous TV sportscasters next door could cover any noise.

Emma thought the glass would never give, but finally it did. She peeled back the tape, carefully inserted her hand into the opening, and unlocked the window.

She dropped her feet to a tiny ledge and grabbed the window frame. With a mighty inner grunt, Emma hoisted the window open and climbed in. Dropping to the floor, she ducked behind an easy chair, trying not to pant.

No time to recover, girl. Do it.

Emma texted Kelly, *I'm in. Second floor.* She crept to the door and peered out. Only one nurse worked at her station mid-floor. With one eye on her, Emma zigzagged toward the end of the hall, checking rooms.

A woman wearing a uniform exited one room.

Aide alert! Emma flattened herself behind a large plant. The aide joined the nurse at the station. Emma held her breath as both walked toward her, then entered a room two doors down. She whipped past the half-open doorway and dashed for rooms on the other end. Emma zigzagged again, listening breathlessly for footsteps as she searched. When she stuck her nose into a room halfway down the hall, her heart exploded.

Dottie Faye.

Eyes closed, her aunt lay in a hospital bed, restraints binding her arms to the rails. Wrath and joy surging through her, Emma darted into the room. She gently removed the restraints and grasped her aunt's warm hand. Dottie Faye stirred, but she didn't open her eyes.

Emma's phone vibrated with an incoming call. Why call instead of text? Frowning, she picked up. "Kelly? I've found ..."

"I'm at the service entrance. It's unlocked!" Her friend sounded strangely cheery. "Meet me here, quick. We'll go in together."

Emma sputtered, "But I told you, I'm already in!"

"Great! I'll see you in a few minutes." Kelly's Pollyanna tone didn't change.

Click.

Something's wrong. Emma went with her gut and called 911. "I think my friend is being held against her will," she pleaded in a low voice. "Behind Maplehurst Senior Community on the Upper West Side. I'm afraid the guy has a gun."

"We'll send officers immediately," the dispatcher's crisp voice answered. "Stay on the line, please."

Emma ached to dash to Kelly's aid, but how could she leave Dottie Faye? She knew she shouldn't linger in the open, but she touched her aunt's soft cheek. Emma scrutinized the room: little furniture; a nearly empty closet; no nooks or crannies in which to hide. She tried to crouch behind a small armchair, but it didn't conceal her. Until Emma knew the police had rescued Kelly, she would hide in the bathroom. She took another long look at her aunt. Then, grasping her can of Mace, she turned on the bathroom light. She pulled off her hat, and out of habit, glanced into the mirror at her hair.

A gun pointed straight at her from behind the shower curtain.

"Great minds run in the same vein, I see." Dr. Giles shoved it aside completely and stepped from the walk-in shower. "Put down that Mace and hand over your phone."

Trembling with anger, she obeyed. The moment the phone left her hand, she realized she hadn't checked messages all day. Had Genetix called?

Would that matter now?

Giles hung up on the 911 operator and pocketed the device. "How fortunate that you charged in while I was washing my hands."

"After 'treating' my aunt?" Emma bared her teeth. "You are the lowest of the low."

"Save your breath." Level green eyes trained on her, Giles gestured with the gun toward the door. "Out of here, please. Slowly."

Emma made her feet move through the doorway. At the sight of white-faced Dottie, her fury burgeoned afresh. Emma's mind ran a manic slide show of futile escape possibilities.

"Don't even think about it." He seemed to read her thoughts. "Your auntie is doing just fine. She's not in pain. But if you don't cooperate, I can change that."

Hot bile rose in Emma's throat, but she nodded.

He waved the gun again. "Walk to the window. Tell me what you see."

She knew better than to lie. "A police car, parked on the street."

He swore. Giles's own phone dinged with a text. He glanced at it and muttered, "Macklin, you idiot. Like I'll drop everything to rescue you."

"What happened to Kelly? What did Reed do to her?" Emma demanded.

"*Quiet.*" He lost all resemblance to the erudite doctor, now masked in the savage face of a hunted man.

Dottie moaned. Emma gripped the windowsill, her knuckles whitening.

Giles growled, "Macklin's probably already spilling his guts about my role in this unfortunate scenario." A look of distaste crossed his face. "Soon the police will converge on this floor. You will tell them you disagreed with me in the past about your aunt's medical treatment, but that we have worked that out. You will say Macklin kidnapped Dottie for her money and brought her here. You were confused about my involvement. I simply have been caring for her, as I would any patient.

"If you say otherwise, remember my gun will be in my pocket—and that I have nothing to lose in using it." His voice, which had softened to an almost silky texture, hardened again. "Do you understand?"

She wanted to claw his eyes out. Instead, she nodded.

"I expect a convincing performance from you, Ms. Cotton." He pocketed his gun, leaving his hand on it. With the other, he touched her arm, and Emma suppressed a shudder. "Let's take a little walk, you and I."

Emma shuffled her feet forward. Dottie Faye murmured restlessly, turning in her bed. *I love you, Aunt Dottie.*

As they walked, Giles pretended to mutter various medical updates on Dottie's condition while Emma tried not to gag at his nearness. They were approaching the nurses' station when a young policewoman bounded from the stairway and trained her weapon on them. "Don't move."

Beside Emma, Giles raised his other hand, his face the picture of bewilderment. "Officer? What's this all about?"

Another policeman joined her. The woman's eyes narrowed. "Sir, we just arrested a man named Reed Macklin who says you helped him kidnap an elderly woman and hide her here."

Giles looked from one cop to the other. "I have no idea what you're talking about. I'm Benton Giles, a physician. I care for a number of patients at Maplehurst."

Gray heads poked out doors up and down the halls. Aides gaped at the scene.

"Stay in your rooms and lock your doors, folks." The policewoman turned to Emma. "Who are you?"

"Emma Cotton." With superhuman effort, she sounded almost natural.

"Ms. Cotton and I were just discussing her aunt's care," Giles said smoothly.

The policewoman demanded, "Do you know anything about this alleged kidnapping?"

Emma feigned outrage. "Macklin abducted my aunt and has been masquerading as her brother so he could steal her money."

"But the head nurse downstairs said a woman also accused Dr. Giles of the kidnapping." The officer's eyes bored into Emma. "Was that you?"

Her next lines caught in her throat, but she forced them out. "I ... was confused. We disagreed on my aunt's medical treatment. I've been so worried about her." Emma let genuine inner trembling color her voice. "I'm afraid I got carried away and said things I didn't mean."

"Ms. Cotton has experienced an immense amount of stress, even more than most caregivers." Giles touched her shoulder, his bedside manner impeccable.

Emma's flesh crawled as she nodded.

A metallic *whang* rang out. Emma jumped and Giles dropped, yelling in pain.

"You stinking, lying Yankee scum!" Dottie Faye, pale but triumphant, smacked his head again with a bedpan.

Emma grabbed it and thunked him herself. "He has a gun in his pocket!" she cried.

The policewoman disarmed the doctor, who lay dazed on the floor, while her partner grabbed the bedpan. "I don't know *what* is going on here, but we'll get to the bottom of this down at the station," the policewoman said. "That's where we're all going. Everyone." She barked into her radio, calling for backup.

Emma clutched Dottie Faye, who nearly collapsed after Giles did. "My aunt is still suffering the effects of the drugs Giles gave her," Emma said. "She needs help—even if she did give him some major lumps." Emma didn't try to keep a tinge of pride from her voice.

A grin fought to curve the officer's mouth. "The EMTs probably are still in the parking area. I called them earlier when we found a woman behind the building."

"Kelly Ann? Where's Kelly?" Dottie Faye babbled.

Dread squeezed the oxygen from Emma's lungs. "Was she all right?"

"Yes. Knocked on the head with a gun, I think, but she'll be all right."

Kelly's alive. Thank You, God. Thank You. If Emma hadn't been holding up Dottie Faye, she would have collapsed too. "May we sit?"

The officer found chairs. The nurse, who had hidden down the hall, began to treat Dottie and Giles. Emma retrieved her phone from the doctor's pocket. She had just breathed her first sane breath in twenty-four hours when it vibrated. "May I answer my phone?"

The officer nodded.

"Hi." Kevin sounded almost happy.

Nice to hear an everyday greeting. "How are things going?" Emma asked.

"Not too bad," Kevin said. "Landon Green tried to strangle me with IV tubing, but Herbie tackled him. I called security. I'd say Landon's on his way to jail."

twenty-three

"Gus and Ida don't look like they would bite you in two, but they could do it." Kevin pointed at the Central Park Zoo's polar bears chest-deep in their pool. The enormous white animals pressed furry, comical faces against the observation glass.

Emma smiled as several small spectators ran to their parents, laughing and squealing. "A good thing to remember about polar bears and people, right?"

"Are you talking about Reed and Giles?" Kevin flashed one of his unfathomable smiles. "Or about me?"

"Maybe all of us."

Another odd smile. Kevin turned and wandered ahead to the penguin exhibit entrance, where Kelly and Dottie waited. Emma took her time, reveling in the newly fallen snow, thick as frosting on Central Park.

She didn't know how she'd bring up the DNA issue today, but that's why they'd planned this time together, wasn't it? To talk it all out, to tie up loose ends and say goodbye before she and Kelly returned to Mystic Harbor?

They visited the comical birds, and then Dottie Faye headed toward the Tropic Zone. "I'm freezing. Let's go inside."

She'd never bonded with Northern winters. Kelly followed, and Emma thought perhaps she could grab the DNA moment she needed. But her mouth went dry when Kevin riveted her with one of his looks. *Oh, no. No, Kevin—*

"Yes," he said softly, "yes, I still care for you. But I understand that's not where you're at."

Though the cold pinched her toes, heat crept up her neck. Moisture formed under her tightly wound woolen scarf. "Kevin, I—"

"I want to be your friend." He touched her shoulder, but didn't grab her hand. "I hope to be more than that someday, but I won't push it. Especially not today."

"Not today," she agreed with a sigh of relief. She hurried to join the others in the Tropic Zone, Kevin behind her, and they all watched monkeys and exotic birds while sweltering in the eighty-degree heat. Resting on a bench, Kevin declared he could stay there all day. The snakes and lizards, however, unnerved Dottie Faye, so they adjourned outside again and walked toward the parking lot. Emma had grown somewhat used to New York's congestion, but she'd never seen this many people in a single area of Central Park. They grouped at the edge of some melee, many holding up phones to take pictures.

"What's going on?" Kelly sprinted ahead and disappeared into the crowd. A minute later, she returned, waving an arm for them to follow. "Snowball fight!" she yelled.

Emma and Dottie dashed after her and broke through the ring of phone-holders to find themselves in the middle of a snowball blizzard. Hundreds of people, mostly young, blurred the air with thousands of snowballs. Emma lost track of how many she threw. She and Kelly held a private snow battle, which ended when Kelly washed Emma's face with snow and Emma stuffed a handful down Kelly's back.

Despite Kevin's limited energy, he surprised Emma with his fearlessness. Like a cannon, he fired snowballs into the crowd and took plenty of hits himself. His germophobia seemed to vanish as he dumped huge armfuls of snow on Emma and Kelly, his eyes glinting with Puck-like mischief.

No wonder. He's wearing gloves. Emma made a direct hit between Kevin's shoulder blades as he turned to escape.

Dottie Faye didn't let her dislike of the cold or her age stop her. With a rebel yell, she gathered armloads of snowballs and attacked indiscriminately.

"We'd better calm her down, don't you think?" Kelly nudged Emma. Kevin grinned.

A group of young men, the target of Dottie's well-aimed assault, raised their eyebrows at each other. Emma read the look in their eyes. How could they clobber an older lady? Even if she fired ammunition like a bazooka!

Emma and Kelly dragged Dottie away with the reminder that Lucinda was expecting them for lunch in a half hour.

Their hostess outdid herself as usual, with fresh seafood chowder, crusty hot bread, cheeses, fruits, and crisp salads. Even Kevin sampled the delicious soup and complimented Lucinda.

She smiled. "I wish your friend Herbie could have come too."

Emma bit her lip. One more casualty from this war of wills. "He's kept to himself since his dad was arrested," she said.

Dottie snorted, "I hope that miserable excuse for a father hasn't ruined his boy's life. I knew Reed Macklin was shady, but I didn't believe he could do such awful things."

"He didn't plan to kill Brett, did he?" Lucinda passed baked Brie cheese topped with almonds.

"No, he meant to kidnap Kevin." Emma grimaced. "Reed confessed that he paid the fake doctor to abduct him from the theater so he could hold him for ransom. Kevin was to remain drugged until Reed, as Kevin's agent and business manager, received the ransom note and paid the money to his own people."

"Ta-dah!" Kelly spread her hands in a grandiose gesture. "Then Kevin would be released unharmed, and Reed would make tons of money and reap the benefits of the publicity generated."

"Instead, the kidnapper mistook Brett for Kevin. When he and Reed figured out they had the wrong actor, Reed killed

Brett rather than let him resurface and possibly disrupt Reed's plans." Emma boiled inside. "I'm glad the police tracked down that fake doctor too. He used his respectable appearance to make a fortune doing other criminals' dirty work, but he blew Reed's assignment big time. Detective Baines told us the police found a ransom note among that thug's belongings, the one Reed had given him to mail."

Lucinda blanched. "Why did Reed come up with such a horrid scheme in the first place? Surely he made plenty of money as a successful agent."

"True," Emma said, "but Reed loved to gamble, and he borrowed from the wrong people."

Kevin said, "I still don't think he meant to hurt anyone—not at first. He just got in over his head."

Seriously? Emma wished they'd clobbered Reed with a bedpan as well.

"Landon was the real surprise," Kevin continued. "He's a better actor than anyone supposed. He hated me, and I hadn't a clue."

Lucinda blinked. "I'm having trouble keeping track of who's who."

"He took Brett's place as my understudy."

"So what was Landon's part in all this?" Lucinda asked, leaning forward.

Emma told her how Reed paid Landon to stun Kevin with a scenery "accident." Though Reed knew nothing about Landon's relationship with Madison, he was well aware of Landon's hostility toward Kevin because he'd beat him out of several starring roles.

Dottie wagged a finger. "The perfect man to smack Kevin upside the head. But that skunk got the wrong guy!"

"He didn't realize Brett was filling Kevin's place at the workshop, and he shoved the scenery from behind. Naturally, he zipped offstage," Emma continued. "Only later did he discover he'd clobbered the wrong actor."

"Too late for Brett, unfortunately. His mother and sister too." Kelly crossed her arms. "And his pastor."

"You would have thought that horrible mistake would have scared Landon onto the straight and narrow," Emma said.

"I wish." Kevin looked at his hands. "No, I guess he saw his chance to knock off the competition."

"He and Madison were so not good for each other." Emma clicked her tongue. "She told the police Landon pressured her to cook poisonous mushrooms in her Thai dish and to argue with Kevin so Landon could switch water bottles."

"Of course, everything was Landon's fault," Kevin said drily.

"To think those two were sneaking around outside a church!" Dottie Faye huffed. "It's a wonder lightning didn't strike them both."

Lucinda set down her coffee cup. "Why did they do that?"

"They didn't want anyone to know they were dating," Kevin explained. "Both their roommates are in theater too—everybody knows everybody in this business. If they'd realized Madison and Landon were a couple, someone might have connected the dots earlier about their anti-Kevin campaign."

"Am I ever glad the police found Landon's fingerprint on both water bottles," Kelly said. "Only one, but that was enough."

"I can't believe he kept my original on his mantel like some sort of trophy." Kevin's brows knitted as he patted a new bottle hanging from his belt.

"He and that swamp slime, Giles, are two of a kind." Dottie Faye shook her fist.

"Landon was out for fame. Reed and Giles wanted money," Emma said. "Gambling sank Reed. Giles's nurse had mentioned that the doctor was in 'terrible trouble.' Apparently, reckless real estate investments sank Giles. They both needed lots of money, fast."

"Not *my* money." They all laughed as Dottie Faye swung both fists for good measure.

"After Brett's death, Reed still needed money desperately," Emma said. "In his eyes, meeting Dottie Faye solved all his problems. She was everything he wanted in a victim. Rich, sweet ...."

"Stupid." Dottie Faye spat out the word. "He thought I was stupid. Why do people like him think they can railroad a woman just because she's over ... forty?"

"That part I have straight. Did Reed really think he could keep you in that nursing home and drain away all your money?" Lucinda asked. "Or was he just looking to make a second kidnapping work?"

Emma didn't doubt Lucinda would have moved the Empire State Building to rescue Dottie Faye. Apparently the cousins were cut from the same cloth. Dottie Faye grasped Lucinda's hand with a grateful look.

Suddenly, though, she snorted. "I don't care why they did it. They should all go to jail for a million years." Dottie Faye smacked the table for emphasis. "Giles stuck a needle in me near the vending machines, when I was buying a snack. It's a good thing Dr. Hart in Mystic Harbor's such a fine Southern gentleman, 'cause if anybody else tries to give me a shot, I'll be ready for him with my bedpan."

Kevin flopped in his chair, gasping with laughter. Emma giggled too, but she had never seen him laugh outright. The unfamiliarity, plus the DNA issue, unsettled her afresh.

"Something wrong, Emma?" Kevin said when he could speak again.

He'd read her emotions. She liked that even less. "Um—"

"Emma Jane never likes goodbyes." Dottie Faye emphasized the last word.

You still think I'm after Kevin. Emma sighed. She made herself look him in the eye. "You need to know something, Kevin. You won't like it."

"I didn't like the attempts on my life, either, but I survived." His glee faded. He straightened. "Say it, Emma."

She took a deep breath. "I not only suspected your involvement in Rose's murder, I obtained a DNA sample from your water bottle and submitted it for analysis to see if it matched what was found under Rose's fingernails."

Pause. "I see."

Two words, but they sliced into Emma. She gripped her hands in her lap.

"I can't think of why the maid hasn't brought coffee." Lucinda beat a tactful retreat.

Kelly blurted, "I helped her, Kevin. In fact, when the courier messed up sending the first sample, I swabbed your mouth when you were asleep and collected another."

Dottie Faye coughed. "Actually, Kevin honey, I got another one, just in case."

"What?" The others stared.

"When?" Kevin bit the word off.

"The day I was kidnapped. I gave you a manicure, remember?" Dottie sounded vaguely insulted. "Fingernails are excellent sources of DNA—"

"Well, well. Aren't you all the crime experts." Kevin's saber-silver eyes stabbed each of them.

Silence.

Emma shuffled her feet. *Say something.*

She couldn't think. Kelly stared at her plate. Even Dottie Faye couldn't seem to force a word out of her wobbling mouth.

"And the results of all these tests?" He ground the words between his teeth.

"Negative," Emma whispered. "You weren't with Rose when she was murdered."

At this point, she had expected ton-size weights to fall from her shoulders. No more hesitation. No more deception.

Instead, the quiet weighed as heavily as her uncertainty had. Emma felt as if she were breathing lead.

"I suppose ..." Kevin seemed to speak to the wall again. "I suppose I should be glad you are such determined detectives."

Did the iron angles of his face relax a smidgen?

"Rose was our friend." Emma raised her chin. "We refuse to call her death an accident."

Kelly straightened her shoulders. "We refuse to let her murderer go unpunished."

"Yes. I understand that you defend your friends. I understand that very well." Kevin paused. "When Landon drugged my water bottle, you were the only ones who believed I hadn't OD'd." He scanned their faces, lingering on Emma's. Hope, like a sputtering candle flame, lit in her.

"You could have grabbed my DNA and run," Kevin continued, "especially when I was—well, a pain."

The understatement of the millennium. Emma read the same fervent assent on Kelly's face.

"Instead, all of you stuck by me. I'll never forget that." His voice broke. Kevin clasped Emma's hand, then Kelly's. Dottie Faye, sitting beside him, threw her arms around him. When he emerged from her hug, a faint grin teased his lips. "Dottie Faye, my offer still stands. I'll never find a more diligent bodyguard than you."

"Call on me whenever you need me, sir." Dottie Faye's face dimpled, then sobered. "I truly wanted to help you pursue the work you love. I still do."

And you still hope he'll promote your acting career. Oh, Dottie Faye.

"We can talk about it." He hinted, "And maybe you could bake me a Granny Whoever's coconut cake?"

"Granny Murleen," Dottie Faye said primly, but her damp eyes shone with gladness. "I just happened to make a quadruple-layer for dessert today."

"And here it is." Lucinda appeared on cue with Dottie's glorious creation.

Later, after they had stuffed themselves, Kevin turned to Emma.

"Did the bad guys—or girl—admit to throwing bricks at you in the parking garage?"

"Surprisingly, no. They've admitted to a lot worse. But no one claims responsibility for that."

"They all deny the emails and messing with the girls' bank accounts and charge cards too." Dottie Faye crossed her arms. "With Reed's and Giles's money problems, I figured they'd found another way to line their pockets."

"But our money is peanuts compared to what they needed," Kelly objected.

"The police don't know if those two crimes are connected at all." Emma tried not to let the stalker sensation creep over her again. But now that she knew Kevin wasn't involved in Rose's murder, Emma wondered how closely the actual killer had been following this New York adventure.

Kevin seemed to read her mind. "I know you won't quit until you solve Rose's murder, and I find that admirable." He looked from Emma to Kelly to Dottie Faye. "Stick together and stay safe."

"We will." Emma echoed Kelly's and Dottie's assurances. Right now, she only wanted to reacquire a sense of normalcy.

"Oh, by the way," Kevin said, turning to Emma, "I did remember what Rose and I argued about."

Emma swallowed. Lately, it hadn't crossed her mind. But now she had to know. "What?"

"We were having a casual conversation, and I mentioned my interest in Shakespeare." His eyes twinkled. "I'd heard Rose was an ardent feminist, so just to annoy her, I told her I liked the strong masculinity portrayed in *The Taming of the Shrew*."

"No wonder she went ballistic!" Kelly exclaimed.

"Not the best way to approach a professor." Emma rolled her eyes.

"Common sense wasn't my forte then." Kevin flashed a mischievous smile. "Still isn't." In a flash, he had become Puck again, but in another, he morphed back to seriousness. "I don't know whether it's significant or not, but I did recall something else about the night Rose died."

They all fell silent. Emma's pulse accelerated.

"I'd procrastinated, as usual, and was racing to finish an assignment due that day, so I didn't leave right after class. When I did, the only student left in the room with Rose was a British guy named Colin." He looked from Emma to Kelly. "Maybe he was the last person to see her alive?"

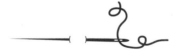

"Guess what?" Kevin, ice skates draped over his shoulder, held up his phone. "Herbie's joining us after all. He'll meet us at the rink."

"Yes!" Emma pumped her fist while Kelly, Dottie, and Lucinda applauded. Maybe Herbie realized he needed a little normalcy too.

When they arrived at the ticket counter, the teen hugged

them all and clung to Kelly. He and Kevin smacked each others' shoulders like ballplayers, then hugged like brothers. Herbie had saved Kevin's life. Perhaps Kevin, in turn, could help fill a void in Herbie's life, guiding him through the theatrical world when his father couldn't.

Kevin had to sign several autographs. "I'm happy to do it," he said, flashing a smile that surpassed his chandelier version.

Emma gasped when they entered the rink. The enormous moonlike surface glimmered, reflecting the actual orb lighting the crystal violet night sky. Hundreds of skaters glided, swirled, and zoomed across the ice, their laughter as loud and joyous as the Christmas music. The luminous New York skyline reached for handfuls of twinkling stars.

Emma hadn't skated in awhile, but the evening's magic guided her feet, and she only hit the deck twice.

Kelly and Dottie Faye skated fearlessly. Kevin took it easy. Herbie and Lucinda turned out to be the champion skaters.

"I've skated at Wollman since I was a teenager," Lucinda said with a shrug after wowing them with a leap and twirl that defied gravity. "Not as agile now, but I'm good for a turn or two."

"I wanted your last night in New York to be special. Does this qualify?" Kevin asked Emma and Kelly as they skated to "Winter Wonderland."

"Absolutely," Kelly said.

"It's incredible," Emma assured him. "Thanks for suggesting it."

He threw a grin over his shoulder as he skated off in a vain attempt to catch Herbie, who had zoomed by and stolen Kevin's hat.

Eventually, Emma pleaded tired ankles. She splurged on hot chocolate with whipped cream while she watched the other skaters and gentle flakes of snow sprinkling the park like sparkles of sugar.

Her mind, however, raced faster than her feet ever could. She'd never envisioned a skaters quilt before, and certainly not like the one taking shape in her head: a landscape with stars, moon, skyline, and the rink, dotted with tiny skater silhouettes—all in black, white, silver, and violet. Wouldn't some of the new metallic fabrics they'd seen in Garment District shops and at the Roman make a gorgeous quilt? Emma pulled her fabric sample book from her bag and drew several rough sketches. She would bounce her idea off Kelly tomorrow as they drove back to Mystic Harbor.

Tonight, though, as she watched her friends laugh and play like children, Emma sipped and celebrated the end of their long, difficult Big Apple adventure.

And she wondered where their new quest would take them.

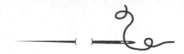

Mystery Sampler Quilt

Create your own mystery sampler quilt with blocks designed by Emma and Kelly and inspired by each book in the series! You'll find a Cotton & Grace block pattern in every Annie's Quilted Mysteries book. At the end of the series, the last pattern will include finishing instructions that will tell you how to stitch the unique blocks together to create a beautiful, one-of-a-kind quilt.

Roman Tiles

Roman Tiles
12" x 12" Finished Block

Specifications
Finished Block Size: 12" x 12"
Skill Level: Beginner

Cutting

From Light Fabric:
Cut 1 (5¼") square.
Subcut square on both diagonals for 4 A triangles.
Cut 2 (4⅞") squares.
Subcut each square on 1 diagonal to make 4 B triangles.

From Medium Fabric:
Cut 1 (5¼") square.
Subcut square on both diagonals for 4 C triangles.

Cut 2 (4⅞") squares.
Subcut each square on 1 diagonal to make 4 D triangles.

From Dark Fabric:
Cut 1 (5¼") square.
Subcut square on both diagonals for 4 E triangles.
Cut 2 (4⅞") squares.
Subcut each square on 1 diagonal to make 4 F triangles.

Assembly

1. Stitch a B and F triangle together along long edge (Figure 1); press seam toward F. Repeat to make two B-F units. Repeat with B and D triangles to make two B-D units referring again to Figure 1.

Figure 1

2. Stitch an A and E triangle together along one short side (Figure 2); press seam toward E. Repeat to make two A-E units. Repeat with A and C triangles and E and C triangles referring again to Figure 2 to make two of each unit.

3. Stitch an A-E unit to a D triangle along long edge (Figure 3); press seam toward D. Repeat to make two A-E-D units. Repeat with A-C units and F triangles to make two A-C-F units referring again to Figure 3.

4. Stitch the remaining E-C units together along long edge matching seams (Figure 4). Press seam open.

Figure 2   **Figure 3**

Figure 4

5. Stitch one each B-D, A-E-D and B-F unit together to make the top row of the block referring to Figure 5 for orientation of units. Press seams in one direction.

6. Stitch two A-C-F units and one E-C square together to make the center row of the block referring to Figure 5 for orientation of units. Press seams in opposite direction of top row.

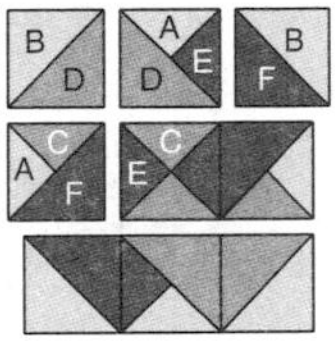

Figure 5

7. Stitch one each B-D, E-B-D and B-F unit together to make the bottom row of the block referring to Figure 5 for orientation of units. Press seams in opposite direction of center row.

8. Stitch rows together matching seams referring to Figure 5 and the block diagram. Press seams open to reduce bulk completing the block.

HELPFUL HINTS

• Choose one light, one medium and one dark fabric for this block. Use scraps from other projects or purchase fat eighths (9" x 22") or fat quarters (18" x 22") to make one sample block.

• Cut individual pieces from scraps, or cut strips and then individual pieces from strips if using yardage or large pieces of fabric. For example, to cut several 2½" squares, cut a 2½"-wide strip the width of the fabric. Subcut the strip into 2½" squares.

Learn more about Annie's fiction books at

AnniesFiction.com

- Access your e-books
- Discover exciting new series
- Read sample chapters
- Watch video book trailers
- Share your feedback

We've designed the Annie's Fiction website especially for you!

Plus, manage your account online!

- Check your account status
- Make payments online
- Update your address

Visit us at AnniesFiction.com